THE GLOW ACROSS THE SEA

THE GLOW ACROSS THE SEA

RYAN M. JONES

This book is dedicated to my wife Shelby,
for being my Light.

PREFACE

I don't remember exactly when, but I believe it happened when I was in middle school. I had a dream that never left me. And while it had no story at the time, the image was powerful. I was in the setting of this book; a dark place full of awful things from which I could not escape. But there was a light off in the distance. And though I couldn't get to it, it was an unmistakable symbol of hope.

And though I'm not sure I really recognized at the time why it was so powerful to me, I always felt that this dream deserved a story. I had tried to write something then, but I didn't get very far before abandoning it.

A few years ago I came back to it after two decades, a little older and a little wiser (though perhaps still young and stupid) and started again. Except for a few of the major elements, it doesn't really resemble what little I'd written years ago, but that's definitely for the best. I'm pleased with how it turned out and I hope others will think it's meaningful.

What I set out to do here was tell a story that was ultimately about love, hope, trust, friendship, goodness, and worth. Any story worth telling ought to have at least some of those elements. And so you'll find them in these pages.

But the other thing I wanted to make sure not to neglect was the very real suffering that we experience in life. The very nature of hope, after all, is that we don't currently have what we hope for. And so while I want to affirm that hope is a good thing, it can also be a difficult thing. And so in this story there's also death, addiction, abuse, poverty, fear, and frustration.

I know that perhaps some of the material may not be suitable for everyone, so read with caution, but I tried to write this in such a way that it could be enjoyed by those as young as early teens all the way to adulthood.

Over the past few years my hope and prayer has been that God would speak through me in this book and in anything else that I write or say or do. The best thing I could ever hope for is for Him to take over more and more. And while allowing Him to do this will be a discipline learned over a lifetime, I believe that by His grace He's spoken here.

Only when it was finished did I start to see how the story could be read from many different angles. All of which draw on stories from my own life; stories that God wrote into me over the course of it, perhaps, at least in part, so that He could weave them into the words of this book.

It's written for the thirteen year old who can't understand the things going on in their mind, for the twenty-one year old who struggles to love and be loved, for the thirty year old who's not always sure where God is, and for anyone else of any age who sits in darkness and hopes for light.

-Ryan M. Jones

CONTENTS

CHAPTER 1

High and Low

Blaise watched the Glow with a sinking heart and heavy, burning eyes. The object of his attention shined brightly and magnificently from a distant area just beyond the horizon and over an onyx black sea. There was no other light like it in his world. It lit up the sky in the distance, but that light didn't fully reach the shore he was on. It provided some light, but only as much as the moon provides in our world. There was a distinct line in the sky where the Glow ended and the darkness began.

For as long as he could remember he wanted to know what the Glow was emanating from, but its source was just barely out of view. To add to his frustration, the waves of the sea raged so violently that it was impossible to cross. He had tried to cross it twice in a rowboat that he'd found and patched up. Eager and determined, he ignored the stories he'd always heard about its impassibility. Though many others had tried to cross the sea, they were either lost to it or didn't get very far

1

before having to turn back. Blaise was the last one in anyone's recent memory to have tried.

"They must not have known what they were doing," Blaise had thought.

The first time, he got about fifty yards from the shore. Then the sea seemed to rage even more violently than usual. Blaise had thought it was just his imagination, but something about it gave him the sense that the sea was truly angry that someone dared venture out upon it. A large wave picked him up. His boat sat on top of its high crest, hurdling him toward the beach before he came crashing down onto it. He hurt himself and the boat, but after he recovered Blaise fixed it and tried again.

The second time was worse. He got about fifty yards out just like the first time when another large wave came to meet him. But this time, instead of riding on top of the wave, it swallowed him up. He remembered tumbling through the water, not knowing which way was up. He woke up on the beach, having very nearly drowned and having aggravated his previous injuries. He hadn't tried to cross the sea since.

He stood on the overlook that pointed to the Glow. It was the closest spot to, it as if built just to point toward it and taunt him. And though he stood on that overlook often, few others ever did. There was a time when the overlook was so crowded that it was hard to get through the hoard to catch a glimpse but not anymore.

Behind him stood the city in which he spent his existence. It was a perpetually dark city - filthy, violent, and dilapidated - and the deeper one ventured into it, the darker it became...Until the Deep Darkness. The Deep Darkness reigned in the reaches of the city farthest from the Glow. Few ever ventured into that impenetrable blackness, and even fewer returned. And on the edge of the Deep Darkness stood three tall, black towers where many resided but of whom little was known.

Blaise's face was blank, and if anything, it was sad, but mostly numb. He ran his thumb across his other fingers, feeling the dirt and grime on them, wondering if they could ever be any other way. He couldn't even think of the word "clean."

As he thought about his dirty hands, another's slim and delicate fingers ran along his forearm from behind and took his filthy hand. A familiar face rested on his shoulder and he rested his head on hers.

"You haven't been out here in awhile," she said.

Blaise sighed. "Even though I get angry when I look at it, I can't seem to stay away when I feel down."

"Do you think anyone's over there?" the girl said.

"I'm not sure, but if there is, they don't seem to care about us. I don't know, Sally. Sometimes I wish it wasn't there at all. I just think if it is there, we should be able to get to it. Maybe that's just a dream."

They paused in silence for a few moments.

"Maybe it's not so crazy," she said before lifting her head off of his shoulder and smiling at him.

"But come on. Let's go."

She tugged on his hand, but before walking from the overlook he looked down at a word graffitied on the ground.

"Glow."

The other words around it meant nothing to him, but he'd once watched who did it. They kept muttering angry phrases, spelling it out as they went.

"G-L-O-W. Glow."

And so that was the only word Blaise could read.

They walked several blocks through dirty streets littered with trash. It was hazy and damp, and they only saw a few street-dwellers meandering around. One was wearing heavy clothing and was sitting on the curb staring blankly at a small fire he'd built on the edge of the street. A few others along the way were stumbling around aimlessly. Blaise and Sally took a wide berth and quickened their pace to avoid them and did the same when they received foul looks from some loiterers standing outside of a building that was known for housing particularly shady business. Not far from their own building, Blaise and Sally saw someone sitting very still against a wall just inside an alleyway. The face wasn't visible because of a hood over their head, but it didn't appear that they were breathing.

"Let's check this out," Blaise said. They walked over and knelt down.

"Hello," Sally said. No response. Blaise picked up a metal pipe that was lying nearby and poked the street-dweller in the side. Still no movement. Sally reached out and checked the wrist for a pulse.

"Nothing," she said, shaking her head.

Blaise slowly pulled the hood off and saw that it was a woman who they'd seen walking in the area recently but hadn't much spoken to.

"Oh no," Sally said under her breath and kneeled down farther to see her face.

"She's got the wide eyes and the half-smile, Blaise. Bright for sure."

Blaise stood up. "That's the third street-dweller we've found dead from it just in the last few sleep cycles."

Sally stood up next to him. "Seems like a lot more of this is happening."

"Understandable I guess," Blaise said.

"It makes it feel like there's a lot more light, and that's hard to come down off of."

They looked down at the poor street-dweller for another few moments. There was nothing they needed to do. The mayor's crews would find her when they made their rounds to gather the dead.

After long enough Sally sighed and said, "Well, it always feels nasty to do this but I guess I better check her pockets." After a few moments of rummaging she stood up and shook her head.

"Nothing. Someone else probably got to her first."

They walked away, crossed the street, and went a couple more blocks before arriving at the doorstep of the old, run-down building where they dwelled. It was a brick building with carved stone work. It had a concrete staircase leading up to the main door. The door was large and had ornate wood carvings in it, though it was badly damaged, and the windows in it had been broken for longer than anyone could remember. It had three floors, all partitioned off into tiny rooms. It was overcrowded and dirty. They walked up the staircase and through the door.

"Evening Mister Blaise. Evening Miss Sally," said the doorman. He kept his eyes on his book and whistled a tune that they thought was a little irritating. Bailey usually sat in his chair reading that same book. It was missing pages, but not only that, it was also missing the ending. Most books in the city, if they were found at all, were damaged, but he never seemed to care.

"Hello, Bailey," said Sally as they continued up the grand staircase to the second floor.

Blaise turned to Sally. "Why does he always say 'evening'? What even is that?"

Sally shrugged. "I'm not sure. I think it has something to do with making sure everything is level. Like if everything's level then it's okay, so it's like saying, 'Everything okay?'"

Blaise laughed. "I'm not sure, but maybe you're right."

Sally gave Blaise a sideways look. "I think that's right because sometimes he says 'mourning' and so I guess that's on a day he's sad. So it makes sense if 'evening' means he's okay."

Blaise shrugged now too. "I see your point, I guess."

Sally patted Blaise on the back. "Plus, don't give him a hard time. He's always done fine watching the door here."

They got to the top of the stairs. Other inhabitants of the building were sitting against the walls in the hallway talking loudly. Some of the children often played a game with rocks they collected. Blaise and Sally didn't know the rules, but from what they could gather, the rules often changed because the children usually disagreed about them more than they were playing the game. They stepped over them on the way to their room.

Blaise shook his head. "I wish this whole building was on the same sleep cycle. It's always so loud when we're about to go to sleep."

Sally nodded in agreement.

Blaise took out his key and unlocked the door. The door

didn't open all the way. It only ever opened about two feet wide before it hit the bed. They just accepted the tediousness of shuffling in sideways through that narrow gap. They closed the door behind them, feeling relieved as the sounds coming from the hallway turned to a muffle.

A wobbly, old chair sat in the corner. Next to the chair was the window, and on the opposite side of that was the storage cabinet for food and other things. The room itself was no bigger than a walk-in closet. Sounds from the other residents of the buildings were ever present.

"Do you hear that?" Sally said. Blaise looked up and perked his ears.

"The neighbors are in a yelling match again. What else is new?" They both heard something shatter, followed by crying. Blaise pounded his fist on the wall.

"Can it over there!"

Sally rolled her eyes at Blaise and took off her tattered, muddy shoes before lying down on the bed. Blaise walked over and took a seat in the chair, propping his feet on the footboard. He looked over at the window and saw a Bright pill on the sill visible in the dim light of a street lamp outside. He'd gotten it the day before and decided not to take it. He didn't like taking Bright, but it was hard to avoid sometimes. After spending some time talking himself out of it, thinking of the Glow and the woman in the street, he laid his head on the back of the chair and closed his eyes. Sally already appeared to be sleeping.

***

Dr. Ambrose looked down at the streets through the floor-to-ceiling windows high from within his penthouse in one of the three towers. He was disgusted by the "street trash" as he referred to them. He hated them. He thought of them as savages.

The wrinkles on his face were deep, and the slant of his brow was harsh and unforgiving. His wire-frame glasses sat uncomfortably on his nose. He stood grimacing, with his hands clasped behind his back, wearing his usual stained and patched tuxedo. Under his feet was a once-pristine and valuable rug, now tattered by ages of wear. Piano music came from a record player behind him. The label on the record was so badly worn that he didn't even know who composed or performed it. It was grand music, but Dr. Ambrose only tolerated it over silence. Despite what was well-done about the music, he was more concerned with what he thought could have been better about it.

The record player sat on an end table with finely crafted woodwork and claw foot legs next to a matching velvet couch, stained and torn in several places.

The grandfather clock chimed, and Dr. Ambrose looked over to see that both hands of the clock were pointed up. Dr. Ambrose turned from the window and walked toward the door of his penthouse. A thin, frail, tower-dweller in a light blue jumpsuit heard the chime as well, knew what that meant, and frantically made his way to the door to make sure that it was open for Dr. Ambrose. Each of them made sure not to make eye contact with the other. Dr. Ambrose went through the opened door with his nose in the air and continued slowly across the slight arch of the bridge. His shoes glided smoothly on the rugs that extended down the hallway. On his right were the lower city, the sea, and the Glow beyond it. On his left was the haunting blackness of the Deep Darkness.

Another tower-dweller was waiting at the door across the bridge and opened it for Dr. Ambrose in a similar manner as the other. He walked through the open door into a penthouse rather similar to his. In the middle of the room sat three high-back chairs made of leather. One was occupied by a man named Kurtz who dwelled in the penthouse of the third tower. He was short, stocky, had a long beard, and a deep voice. Another chair was occupied by Wilkins, the master of the three towers, and the resident of the penthouse in the middle tower where the three met regularly. He sat in his robe, slippers, and slicked back hair.

Dr. Ambrose walked over to his chair and sat down. Kurtz then signaled with a hand gesture to the three guards in the room. They carried old clubs with several nails hammered through each of them and thick padded gear. Upon seeing the signal, the three guards took up their respective posts next to each entrance; one by the elevator, one by the door to the bridge to Dr. Ambrose's tower, and one by the door to Kurtz' tower. Dr. Ambrose leaned forward, eager to say what was on his mind.

"Well Wilkins, what will convince you?"

"Ambrose, Ambrose, my dearest Ambrose," Wilkins said with a smirk. "We have all the luxuries in the world. Our existence is grand. The trash down there on the streets is none of our concern."

Dr. Ambrose frowned.

Kurtz then interjected. "Come on, Ambrose, there's no

need to throw away Watchers in order to further this silly crusade of yours. Sure, they're garbage down there, but all you're doing is more than enough to keep them weak and out of the way. Leave it alone. They're not worth any more time."

Ambrose remained tense and silent.

Wilkins started again, "Can we please put this topic to rest, Ambrose? Please. It's exhausting."

Ambrose threw himself back in his chair. "But you know as well as I do that if we don't eradicate or control the street scum, they'll always pose a risk. They envy us, and it's only a matter of time before they become even more of a nuisance than they already are."

"There's no support from the Citizens," said Wilkins. He continued with a dark coolness in his voice. "If we send Watchers to wipe them out, that'll leave us vulnerable, and they'll sense it. They're not as dull as I'd like. I'll not sacrifice comfort. Comfort is what keeps the three of us where we are. Remember, comfortable subjects equals comfortable kings." Kurtz sat back in his chair nodding in agreement.

Wilkins turned to Kurtz, "What news on that other matter?"

Ambrose just continued to scowl.

Kurtz answered. "Nothing notable to report. We took care of that instance of insubordination. It's nice to have one of those incidents every so often. We made an example out of the little weasel. I'll not expect the others to get any ideas after they all watched him stand on the top of the tower and become street scum a single moment later."

Wilkins and Kurtz let out a sinister laugh. Dr. Ambrose would have too, but he was still frustrated. He was consumed with his desire to end the street trash. He felt that the one blemish on the society of the towers was that they were allowed to exist alongside it. Getting rid of them meant that the world would be perfect. But without the support of Wilkins and Kurtz, and therefore the Watchers, there would be no assault.

As the other two talked, he got up from his chair and began walking back to the bridge to his penthouse. Wilkins and Kurtz were still laughing to each other about their cruelty and didn't acknowledge him as he left. The tower-dweller in the light blue jumpsuit dragged open the door as the Watcher stood tall and proud next to it. Dr. Ambrose acknowledged neither as he walked through and onto the bridge. His head was bowed slightly and he was moving slowly as he continued over the bridge. He glanced at the streets but then quickly turned his gaze to the Deep Darkness.

The tower-dweller in the light blue jumpsuit opened the door to his penthouse and he went through. It was silent and lonely, but he felt more at ease than with the others. He continued his march toward the elevator door, and upon arriving, he pressed the call button. Even in his dark room, it still only gave off a dim light. With the dissonant twang of a decrepit bell, the elevator door opened unsteadily like an elderly gentleman rising from his chair. He took out his key and placed it in the keyhole and pressed the unmarked button about halfway down.

The elevator started with a jerk and then moved down for some time. The elevator then slowed and made a screeching noise before it came to a clunky stop. The door opened unsteadily again, and Dr. Ambrose began to squint. He stepped out of the elevator into what was likely the best lit room in the entire city.

The Bright laboratory took up an entire floor. It was filled with harsh, artificial lights and had no windows. Here there was a large number of tower-dwellers in light blue jumpsuits all working feverishly. More Watchers with bats were overseeing them, making sure the lab remained secure. There were several long rows of tables, all with different equipment.

He continued down one of the aisles looking to his left and right, taking stock of the operation. Dr. Ambrose passed one worker and noticed that the worker was carelessly mixing chemicals and not at all paying attention to the ratios Ambrose had clearly set. He scowled at him, the worker oblivious to his displeasure. He waved a Watcher over and pointed at the worker's back. Dr. Ambrose kept moving down the aisle observing other parts of the operation.

The Watcher approached the wayward worker and didn't hesitate to hit him hard in the head with a club. The worker toppled to the ground, and the other Watchers gathered around and dragged him out of a side door. The other workers paused briefly in shock before getting back to work even more fervently. Dr. Ambrose made his way to the back of the room and entered his office. He slowly closed the door, looking back into the laboratory that he had worked so hard to build, displeased by the constraints upon him. To Dr. Ambrose, the sound of the latching office door sounded like the latching of a cage. He sat brooding at his desk. Each of his own thoughts made him angrier and angrier until an idea came to his mind.

"Yes...Yes...that could work!" His rage was now redirected

from Kurtz and Wilkins and back onto the street trash. He took out a piece of paper and a pen and began writing. A knock at the door interrupted him.

"WHAT!?"

The door creaked open and a face appeared, but the rest of the body stayed outside. "Do...do you require anything Dr. Ambrose? Your usual tea perhaps?"

Dr. Ambrose glared back at him. "Will you prepare it correctly this time?" The face nodded in understanding and began to close the door.

"Wait!" The door opened again and the face reappeared. He finished his scribbling, folded the paper, and sealed it in an envelope. Dr. Ambrose slid it toward the front of his desk. "Make sure this gets to our man below."

CHAPTER 2

Survival

Blaise didn't feel like he had his eyes closed long before he heard a knock at the door. He was sleepy, but he rubbed his eyes and got out of his chair. He opened the door just slightly before the man on the other side forced his way in. He was thin, malnourished, and looked sickly. His eyes were sunken into his head. Blaise recognized that look. It was one of a fully-fledged Bright addict. Blaise fell back onto the bed which in turn woke Sally.

"What was that all about?" yelled Blaise.

"I thought we were trying to sneak into that house, but you two didn't show up. It's been sitting unguarded for a while now and we need to go," responded the sickly man.

"Fine. We're getting up, Parker, but there's no need for that kind of entrance next time," Sally said as she swung her feet off of the bed.

"Look, I'm sorry, but we need to go," said Parker.

Blaise stood up again and yawned. "Alright, lead the way, but then I'm going back to sleep."

The three shuffled out of the room and hurried down the stairs. Bailey was asleep in his chair as they continued out the door. They walked at a quick pace around the corner of the building and into the alleys.

"This should be a pretty straightforward job," said Parker. "This group is small like us, but they somehow got a lot of Bright. More than anyone should have their hands on."

"How did you find out about this again?" Sally said.

"Overheard it when I was walking around at the Arena. They thought they were talking quietly, but not quietly enough. I was hiding around a corner. Followed them back to their place from a distance and started casing it."

"Okay. So what's the plan then, Parker?" Blaise said.

"Yeah, so there's a small window near the ground that leads into the basement where the stuff is. I was thinking since Sally is the smallest, she'll have to slip in and then hand it all to us. Then we pull her out and run and hope they never realize we were there."

"What!?" Sally said, almost before he could finish. "So, since I'm taking all the risk, I should get the bigger cut, right?"

"Even share every time. That's always been the deal," said Blaise.

"How am I supposed to rely on you two to pull me back out if someone shows up?"

"Well no one better show up then," said Parker.

Sally rolled her eyes.

Parker continued. "I've tracked their sleep schedule and

they should be sleeping pretty soundly right now. That's why we need to get this done."

"I always hate these schemes," said Sally. "I wish we could figure out another way to survive."

Blaise nodded his head in agreement. "Well we've certainly tried. Growing food to sell hasn't worked for us. Everything dies."

"I don't know why you two hate this so much," said Parker. "Dealing in Bright is so much more interesting than some gross cabbage."

"Maybe it's more interesting," said Sally, "but it's more stressful. I feel like I'd actually be helping by growing food rather than doing this."

"Helping!?" said Parker. "This is helping. Everyone down here wants Bright. What else is there for us?"

Blaise shrugged. "I don't know. I guess I want...something more."

Parker gave Sally and Blaise a perplexed look. "You two spend too much time looking at that ridiculous Glow. There is nothing more. Do what you need to survive, and take Bright until you die. That's what I think. What's the Glow ever done for us here?"

Blaise dropped his head and shook it. He didn't really want to argue about it, especially since he was inclined to feel the same way at the moment. "Well, anyway, how much farther is this place?"

"Far enough," said Parker. "I was actually glad that I had to follow them pretty far away. We don't know them, and they don't know us, so it's unlikely they'll ever know what hit them."

Blaise looked around at the broken down row houses. "Yeah, I'm not familiar with this area now."

"Right," said Parker.

Blaise was hanging his head and not saying anything. Parker looked over at him, noticed his gloomy appearance, and thought he should say something.

"What...what do you guys think they have in the Towers? Do you think they know how to get to the Glow?"

Blaise looked up at him. "That's always been a rumor, but I think it's just speculation or wishful thinking or whatever."

Parker scratched his head. "You're probably right. I imagine whatever they have, they're much better off though. A lot happier than we are down here I'm sure."

"Yeah I guess that at least is right," said Blaise.

Parker then suddenly shushed the conversation.

"We're close. Be quiet." After passing another building, Parker pointed out the window that sat near the ground.

"I don't see any lights. I think we're okay." He kneeled down and slid the panel open.

"Ok, Sally, you're up."

"I swear, this better be worth it," she said in a hushed voice. After a momentary pause she slid her feet down into the basement.

"Where is this stuff?" she whispered.

"Back wall," Parker said, trying to keep his voice down. She returned with a large can filled with Bright, more Bright than any of them had ever seen at one time. Parker and Blaise's eyes widened at the sight. They put it aside.

"There's another large can with some..." Parker was cut short. There was noise on the floor above the basement.

"Leave it! Get to the window, Sally!" said Blaise. Blaise and Parker grabbed each of Sally's arms and tried to pull her out. The door of the basement opened, and just as they got her out, a hand grabbed her ankle and started pulling her back in. Sally started kicking with her other foot, but was slowly getting dragged back. Parker and Blaise looked at each other, and Blaise didn't like the look in Parker's eyes.

"Sorry. At least one of us ought to survive this." Parker then let go of Sally's hand, grabbed the can of Bright and took off back down the street. Blaise held on, but was losing ground.

"Pull!" yelled Sally, but she kept getting dragged in.

At one moment, Blaise thought about just letting go and running off too, but he knew that finding another companion on the streets wouldn't be the same. They'd learned to work well together and without her, most of the jobs and stunts they'd pulled wouldn't have been successful. She was an irreplaceable resource, and he needed her back. So Blaise pulled harder, and Sally was able to get a grip with her other foot and break the hold of the hand in the basement holding her in. They stumbled to their feet and took off back in the direction of their building.

After running for a while, weaving through different alleys and streets, and confident that they hadn't been followed, Sally slowed down.

"Can we stop for a second?" She put her hands on her scraped up knees and tried to catch her breath.

"That snake Parker just cut and ran. He left us there," she said.

"Typical," said Blaise, not wanting to reveal to her that

he briefly thought about doing the same. She stood back up and took a couple steps forward before her leg gave out. The adrenaline had kept her from realizing how hurt she was, but now that it had worn off, she could barely walk.

"Come on, Sally, no time," said Blaise.

"I can't walk! Help me up!" yelled Sally. Blaise rolled his eyes, but leaned down to help her up. He put her arm over his shoulder to act as a crutch, and they continued slowly the rest of the way back.

It was a long slow-going walk that felt like it would never end. Blaise was irritated at the extra burden but he just kept his mind on getting back to their building. They eventually arrived and struggled up the front steps. As soon as they got in the door, Bailey hopped up to help, noticing that Sally was hurt.

"What can I do for you, Miss Sally? Let's get you seated." Bailey took Blaise's place under her arm and sat her down in his chair. He went back into his room behind his desk and came back with a bag of ice.

"Where's it hurt?" he said.

"My ankle," she said grimacing. He placed the ice pack on it, and she grimaced at that too but then started to relax.

"That's helping. Thank you, Bailey," Sally said. Blaise stared and wondered what Bailey's motivation might be. Anyone who was a little too helpful in the dark city was worthy of suspicion. Did he have some angle? Did he expect something in return? But the longer Blaise waited and watched, Bailey never showed the slightest sign of having a catch. Blaise stood puzzled at the whole exchange. There had never been more than surface pleasantries between any of them, and he'd never seen the old bag of useless books and wrinkles do anything but sit in that same chair.

"Who are we to him?" Blaise thought. Sally looked comfortable and possibly sleeping in the chair, and Bailey sat on a stool in the corner intent on looking after her. Confused but satisfied, he continued up the stairs to the room. He opened the door and slid in the room sideways as always. He closed the door and took a seat on the bed.

"Wonder where Parker went," he thought. *"Better show up again soon."*

***

Blaise woke up again sometime later. Sally was asleep next to him, breathing softly, her exhales brushing against his face. He wasn't sure how she got there, but he was glad that she was. He lifted his head and saw her ankle wrapped tightly with bandages and still propped up by an ice pack. Sitting in the chair was Parker. He was staring at the ceiling. He had a half smile, his eyes were wide, and he was breathing heavily and sweating.

Parker was oblivious, but Blaise still shook his head and glared at him before laying back down on the pillow and staring at the ceiling, contemplating. Most of the things he saw in the dark city just made it feel darker. But then some things, like the way Bailey acted, reminded him of the Glow. He couldn't describe it really, but things like that made the Glow feel a little more reachable, and the sea a little less vengeful.

Blaise dozed off again and woke up some time later not

realizing he'd fallen asleep. Parker was standing over him, trying to get him and Sally up. A bag was over his shoulder.

"Come on. Wake up. We have to get to the Arena and sell this stuff sooner rather than later."

It was always difficult to get out of bed in the dark city. There, the only drug more widely used to numb the pain than Bright was unconsciousness. Blaise was on his stomach and propped himself up on his elbows to rub his eyes. Sally was on her back and stirred awake too. Her eyes were red and watery from drowsiness and the pain in her ankle.

"Let me try and put some weight on this foot," she said. She slowly moved her feet to the floor and tried to stand up. She got up slowly and then started to stand up straight, grimacing as she stood.

"Still sore, but I think the swelling went down. I think I can walk." She took a couple steps, grimaced again, but kept moving.

"I'm alright," she said, "but let's keep it slow."

They all shuffled out the door to the room and headed down the steps. Sally was moving with a limp and clutched the handrails as she went, but was otherwise unaided. Blaise and Parker moved rather quickly down the sidewalk, looking back exasperated at Sally who couldn't keep up.

"Let's go, Sally!" bellowed Blaise in a harsh tone. She didn't respond. She shook her head, let out a sigh, and kept moving.

They soon came to an old, domed building. Several other street-dwellers were heading into one of the heavy metal doors that led inside. They waited for a few others to file in and then went through the doors themselves.

Blaise, Sally, and Parker walked in to find throngs of other street-dwellers yelling over each other. "The Arena," as it was called, was a hub for the street-dwellers. It hosted different sports and other entertainment down on the floor. Currently there was a boxing ring set up in the middle, and by his bloodied face and drooping shoulders, one competitor appeared to be close to defeat.

Along the concourse above were numerous stalls and tables for trading weapons, food, Bright, and almost anything else. Shopkeepers and patrons were not-so-nicely shouting at each other trying to negotiate deals. Others were just filing by looking at what there was. The three began walking around the concourse.

At one point, Parker went over to a particular stall without saying anything to Blaise and Sally. All Blaise and Sally could see was Parker opening the bag that he had brought and the shopkeeper's wide eyes as he peered into it. The shopkeeper quickly took it and ducked down under the counter. After a few moments, the shopkeeper stood back up, handed the bag back to Parker, and dropped something else in his hand. Parker walked back over to Blaise and Sally and handed them some grubs.

"A little bit of high-class cuisine in exchange for some of the latest haul," he said. He then opened the bag for them and they all looked in to see a pile of beat up coins of different shapes and colors. They didn't look at all like how they had originally, and the markings were entirely unrecognizable.

"Wow," said Sally. Then looking at Blaise she said, "We might be able to get a bigger place with this."

Blaise just stared in shock for a moment before saying "I think you might be right."

Parker closed the bag and slung it over his shoulder. "Don't go spending it all just yet. Remember, a third of it is mine."

"I think you mean to say that *all* of it is *ours*?" said a voice over Blaise's shoulder.

Blaise and Sally watched Parker gulp before they turned and looked. Standing there was a group of five street-dwellers, all much taller and stronger than them.

"You think we didn't get a look at your faces? And now we see you here selling our stuff?"

Blaise and Sally backed toward Parker. Parker backed up even farther.

"Come on, we can work this out," Parker said, still moving away. The leader of the other group moved Blaise and Sally to either side and the whole group of five moved toward Parker. The leader grabbed him by the shirt and pulled him in.

"Okay, Okay, Okay. Just take it!" Parked shrieked. "I didn't mean anything by it. I was just trying to survive just like everybody out here. Please don't hurt me. Come on. Just take it and go on, and we'll never bother you again."

Parker held out the bag, and the leader took it with his free hand before throwing Parker to the floor. The leader glared at each of them for a moment before signaling to the others and disappearing into the crowd.

Parker stood up and went over to Blaise and Sally looking embarrassed. "Well, so much for that I guess. At least we didn't get beat up."

Blaise dropped his head and clenched his fists. "Every time something that isn't bad happens...."

Sally put her hand on Blaise's back, but didn't know what to say. Blaise sighed and lifted his head. "It's fine. Just how it is here. No point in dwelling on it."

They started walking around the concourse, and after having done a full lap, they saw that the bloodied man was being dragged out, and the victor was walking away with his arms up receiving the cheers. Another quickly climbed into the ring and yelled loudly and abrasively, "The meeting is about to start!"

"Meeting?" Blaise said as they all looked at each other. "Did either of you know about a meeting?"

"No," said Sally and Parker almost in unison.

Many of the street-dwellers started toward the seats. Others acted like they didn't hear the announcement and kept moving around the concourse. Blaise, Sally, and Parker found a spot at the top of an aisle and stood there waiting. No one seemed to know the purpose of the meeting. There was plenty of murmuring and shoulder-shrugging going on all over the Arena.

Mayor Max then stepped out of the tunnel, followed by a number of his guards. The room came to a hush. He stepped up into the boxing ring dressed in an old pinstripe suit. He surely wasn't a young man, but not so elderly either. He was bald and a little chubbier than most of the other street-dwellers and though he wasn't an official leader, he certainly had a lot of influence whether he deserved it or not. Hungry for guidance, even if it was poor, many street-dwellers hung on his every word.

"Greetings!" he cried in a jolly voice. The crowd cheered, and Parker joined in. Blaise and Sally clapped lightly.

"I've called everyone here today to discuss our liberation!" He held both hands high in fists, and the crowd roared even louder, though still unsure as to what he was referring to. Blaise and Sally exchanged concerned glances.

Mayor Max continued. "Those in the towers would look down on us, but we're stronger than they are!" More cheers. "We are tempered by the fire of our plights, while they sit upon their thrones of luxury, softened into weakness by their comforts. They keep food for themselves, while we struggle to survive."

He took a long pause and circled the ring looking at the street-dwellers. Then, starting out quietly and building into a great crescendo, he yelled, "The time has come to build an army!" The cheers were louder than anyone had ever heard in the Arena. "And then we will storm the towers and take what we deserve!"

Cheers rang out and as they continued, Blaise and Sally remained unmoved, staring intently at Mayor Max and occasionally glancing at one another.

Mayor Max pointed at a big clock high up on the wall. "We will meet here again in one cycle of the small hand, and then our revolution will begin."

After that final statement, Blaise looked at Sally and Parker, made a motion with his head to indicate that he wanted them to follow, and turned toward the nearest door. The three stepped outside. The door closed behind them, and they could still hear the muffled cheers inside.

"This is bad," said Blaise. "Everyone who goes to the towers will be killed."

"Why does Mayor Max all of a sudden think this is the right idea?" said Sally.

Parker threw up his hands. "What's wrong with you two? This isn't bad news. A lot of us may get killed, but it might be worth a shot. Think of existing with all the great things they must have up there."

"But no one down here understands how they do things," Sally interjected. "Just because the tower-dwellers know how to work the things they have, doesn't mean we'll know how to use them. Then we'll be in real trouble when we starve."

Parker looked indignant. "We could figure it out. We're as smart as they are."

"Are you willing to bet your existence on it?" Blaise said. "Remember the last time someone tried to attack the towers? Several groups banded together and were killed. And even worse, they were dropped in a pile outside the Arena as a warning. Provoke the towers again and who knows what they'll do. We need to stop this. But how?"

"Could we try to convince Mayor Max to stop it?" Sally said.

Blaise shrugged. "Probably not. He doesn't take suggestions from anyone who isn't in his inner circle."

There was a long pause. Parker looked annoyed, and Blaise and Sally both looked around, thinking. As Blaise stared at a pothole in the street, Sally started talking again.

"We...we could go warn the towers," she said.

Blaise looked at her. "So...what? Just walk up to the towers and expect them to listen to us?"

"It's our only shot," responded Sally. "If we say we're trying to help, maybe they won't hurt us. If we can warn them, we may be able to avoid disaster. Maybe we can talk about getting along."

The word "peace" was the right one, but they didn't know it.

"Well, let's go then," said Blaise. "No time to lose."

Blaise and Sally took two steps before Parker interrupted their stride. "Wait, wait, wait. Are we really actually doing this?"

"Weren't you just all excited about trying to attack the towers? So you'd attack them, but won't go there to help us stop them?" asked Blaise.

"Well I mean...I'm just saying that maybe we should stop and think. I mean it's not so bad down here, right? Maybe attacking them is too risky, but so would be going to warn them. So maybe let's do neither."

Sally stared at him. "So then it's all talk with you?"

"I...I...umm."

"Come on Parker, we can use your help." Blaise said.

Parker grumbled. "I don't like this, but okay. Let's just get back as fast as we can."

Sally smiled. "You like sneaking more than fighting anyway, Parker, so it should suit you."

They started walking away at a brisk pace. Blaise furled his brow thinking of the terrible things that could happen. War really starting between the streets and the towers would be a big enough problem. But he was also concerned about what could happen to them just by trying to enter those forbidden skyscrapers. There was, however, another thought that propelled him forward:

"What if they really do have a way to the Glow?..."

CHAPTER 3

Shadowlands

Blaise, Sally, and Parker were moving through the streets and alleys of the city getting ever closer to the three towers. The farther they went away from the shore, the darker and dirtier it got. Few street-dwellers ventured anywhere close to the towers, and even fewer actually spent their existence in these shadowy areas. As they went along they saw flickering lights reflecting on some buildings from around a corner.

Sally leaned toward Blaise. "Is that...a campfire?"

Sally snuck up to look around the corner. "It *is* a campfire!" She tried to whisper it, but then covered her mouth realizing that she might have been too loud. But after a moment, she turned to look back and gave a report. "There are some odd-looking street-dwellers sitting around it. They're just wide-eyed and staring," she said.

Blaise moved up closer to Sally "Do they look dangerous?"

Sally shrugged. "I don't know."

"Maybe we shouldn't find out," said Parker. "Maybe we should find a different way around."

Blaise thought for a moment.

"We could find another way, sure, but it's harder to see out here, and with that campfire we can see almost all the way to the towers. I say we take our chances."

"I think you're right. I'll follow you," said Sally. Parker looked less convinced but agreed.

Blaise peeked around the corner himself to get a glimpse and waved to Sally and Parker. The three stepped out from behind the corner and moved toward the campfire. They didn't dare move quickly. Sally reached out and put her hand on Blaise's arm so as to have him escort her. Blaise felt a little annoyed at first, but he stood up a little taller because of it.

They inched closer, and they could tell that there were five street-dwellers sitting on the ground around the fire. They wore clothes even more tattered than what Blaise, Sally, and Parker were used to seeing. Their shirts were so ripped that they might as well not have worn them. Their unkempt beards went in all directions, and what parts of their faces weren't covered by facial hair were caked in soot. They slowed down, certain they would be noticed as they got closer. But they weren't. Blaise, Sally, and Parker were just feet from the back of one of them when they stopped. Blaise looked at Sally. He then took another slow step closer. Sally let go of his arm and Blaise took a couple more steps until he was right behind one of them.

"He..Hello," he said.

In an instant all five faces turned to stare directly at Blaise, Sally, and Parker. One of the campfire men started to make a growling noise through his teeth, and then they all started to scowl. The growling man, in a gargled voice as though his throat hadn't been cleared in ages, yelled "AAGHRS! AAAAGHRSS!" Blaise, Sally, and Parker took a step back.

"I...I think he's trying to say 'ours'," said Sally. Blaise, Sally, and Parker began to move slowly around the fire, making sure not to turn their backs on them. The five men's eyes followed them in an eerie unison the whole time. As Blaise, Sally, and Parker got to the other side, they began backing up, still keeping their faces toward the men.

Feeling as though they were clear, they turned to run. But just as they did they were met by several other men walking toward them who looked the same as the others.

"Uhh Blaise," said Sally. "What should we do?"

"Maybe...let's...turn around." They all did so and saw that the ones sitting around the campfire had now stood up and were walking toward them as well.

Parker nearly collapsed in fright. "Any other ideas?"

Blaise looked around frantically and saw an open door to a rundown building through a gap in the growing number of campfire men. He grabbed Sally's hand and took off. Parker followed. They ran up the stairs and into the door. There they were met by even more campfire men who were stirring awake from different places all over the floor. They turned to go back, but there were already campfire men on the stoop.

"Up the stairs!" Blaise said, and the three went as fast as they could up to the second floor. There didn't appear to be any campfire men up there as they quickly split up to look into each of the three rooms.

Parker yelled from one room, "The fire escape was in here, but it's collapsed."

Blaise looked around the room that he was in and saw nothing useful. There were some old clothes and piles of other junk. Parker ran into Blaise's room as the campfire men were slowly making their way to the second floor. His eyes were wide, and he looked helpless.

"What do we do?"

Sally then ran into the room, almost knocking Parker down. She was holding a small cardboard box, shrugging and shaking her head.

"All I found were these matches."

Parker and Sally realized that the campfire men were now right behind them. They moved quickly over to Blaise, and all three of them backed into the far corner of the room that was now filling up with wild-eyed campfire men.

"What now?" Parker said.

Sally was hiding behind Blaise's shoulder. "Blaise...Blaise..."

Blaise was having a hard time thinking, and time was running out, but he was able to think of one longshot idea.

"Sally. Give me those matches."

"Okay." Out of nervousness though, she fumbled them in her hands. As Blaise tried to grab them, he accidentally batted the whole box over toward the campfire men.

Blaise didn't have time to debate with himself. He took a deep breath and plunged toward it. He grabbed the box, but all Parker and Sally could see after that was the campfire men closing in around him until they could no longer see him.

"Blaise!"

The campfire men looked as though they were about to

pounce on him. Sally was about to run in to try and help when all the campfire men backed up slightly. A flicker of light was bouncing off the walls. Parker and Sally saw Blaise stand up holding a single lit match, each of the campfire men now completely mesmerized by it.

Keeping his eyes on the match and the men, Blaise waved for Parker and Sally to come over to him. They hesitated, but to their surprise, they were now inches from the campfire men without them appearing to notice. The match went out, and for a brief moment the campfire men were angry again. Parker and Sally almost ran back to the corner, but Blaise quickly lit another match, and they were mesmerized again.

Step by step and match by match they made their way down the stairs and out of the building. Once they were out of reach of any campfire men, Blaise threw down the box of matches, and they all ran as quickly as they could away and toward the Towers.

After a while they stopped to catch their breath, still shaken.

"What was wrong with them?" asked Parker. "Were they Deep Ones?"

"No, I don't think so. But they've definitely spent too much time in the shadows," Blaise answered.

"I've heard stories of what can happen the deeper in you get," said Sally. "But I'm not sure I believed it until just now. And we're not even in the Deep Darkness."

"But we're right on the edge of it," Blaise said. "Sometimes real Deep Ones come out of the Deep Darkness, but not often. The stories I've heard will chill you to your bones."

Parker gulped. "Don't tell any. I don't want to hear them.

I've heard before that anyone who's ever gone into the Deep Darkness has never come back. Some say that anyone who goes in becomes a slave to the Deep Ones. Others say you become a Deep One yourself. I want as little to do with it as possible."

They all went silent for a moment.

"Well I guess we better keep moving," said Sally. She took a step forward, winced, and reached down to rub her leg.

"I think I hurt my ankle again running like that."

She took another few steps limping some, but moving well enough.

"I think I'll be alright, but I need to be more careful."

They started walking and realized that they were practically there. The three towers were only a couple of blocks away. It was disorienting to look straight up at them, but it was an awe-inspiring sight that none of them had seen up close before. They reached about as high as they could see. The darkness this far in felt thick as it seemed to envelope the towers, and the only reason they could really see the towers at all was because of some of the dim lights that came through the windows. The question now, however, was how to get in.

"That tower to the right looks darker than the other two," said Blaise. "It might be easier to sneak in through there."

"I think you're right," agreed Parker. They made their way quickly and carefully toward that tower. But they stopped abruptly when they saw someone ahead of them walking toward the main entrance. It was just a dark outline of a human. They couldn't really see anything meaningful. But the shadowy figure saw them too, and started walking in their direction. Blaise, Sally, and Parker took a step back, but were too frightened to run.

When the figure was close they heard it say in a soft-spoken girl's voice, "Nice to see new folk about. Are you coming to visit the towers?"

She then stepped close enough for them to see her. Her head was shaved and she was wearing a light blue jumpsuit. She looked thin and frail, but was about the same age as them. There were bags under her eyes, but she gave them a warm smile, and they felt at ease. They noticed too that she repeatedly tried to make eye contact, but always averted her eyes after each attempt.

Sally piped up.

"Well, yes actually. Who are you?"

"I'm an Attendant in the towers," the girl answered.

"But sometimes I like to come down to the streets, and if I happen to meet someone who wants to come in and see the towers, I may or may not have my ways of organizing a visit."

Blaise, Sally, and Parker looked at each other and shrugged.

"What are your names?" the girl asked.

"I'm Sally. This is Blaise, and this is Parker."

The girl smiled and nodded. "Nice to meet you," she said.

"What's your name?" said Sally.

"I don't really have a name. My number is '923.'" She turned and pointed to the number on the back of her jump-suit."

Blaise, Sally, and Parker all had questions, but didn't think it was the time to ask. Parker started to say something before Blaise elbowed him in the side.

"What?"

"Save it. Let's just get in the towers."

923 had already turned and started walking. "Well, come on. Let's go," she said as she turned back to see if they were coming. The three didn't know if it was a trick, but 923 seemed sincere. They walked across the empty street and then around to the side of the building.

"There aren't many Watchers guarding this tower," 923 said. "This is the tower where the Attendants dwell. But we do have to go up a back stairwell. Parts of that staircase collapsed a long time ago, so there is some climbing to do, but the Watchers don't guard it because of that. Come on."

As they continued around the side of the building, Blaise, Sally, and Parker were startled by the thick and intimidating Deep Darkness that stood in front of them. It was so black it appeared as though it were truly the absence of any existent thing. True nothing. None of them had ever been that close to it, and none of them immediately realized how wide their eyes were and how far their jaws had dropped. They each took slow steps toward it.

"Wow," Blaise said in a hushed tone. They all got goosebumps and chills. Sally came up next to him and took his hand. Blaise held onto it tightly. They could see the Deep Darkness from the streets, but seeing it from there and seeing it up close were two different experiences.

923 stopped with them momentarily, apparently unphased by it, and then kept walking further. Each step closer for Blaise, Sally, and Parker was daunting. Terror drove through them like a knife with each passing step. To their relief, 923 stopped at a broken window. She stuck her head in it, looked around, and then proceeded to climb through.

"This way," she said from inside the building. Blaise and Parker helped Sally up. 923 helped soften her landing on the other side. Parker then hoisted himself up and through. Blaise stepped up to the window, looked at the Deep Darkness again, felt another chill, then turned away and proceeded up and in too.

Once inside, they found themselves in a small room. There was trash and rubble all over the floor and a lone desk and chair in the middle of the room. They stepped through the debris and out the door into a hallway. 923 led the way, weaving through several different hallways. None of the others could have known how to find their way back out. Blaise felt a bit uneasy about that, and a number of bad thoughts came to him.

"What if this is some trick and 923 is just someone sent down here to lure unsuspecting victims into servitude? What if we're being led to our deaths?"

But at this point he knew they were committed. For better or worse, they didn't have much choice but to go with her. 923 stopped at a door. She started jiggling the door knob and was putting her shoulder into it.

"This is my favorite spot in the whole building," she said as she continued to try to get the door open.

"No worries," she said. "This door is a little tricky, but I can get it."

After a few more moments, 923 put her shoulder into it one more time, and the door screeched open, the bottom of it scraping across the floor. It didn't open far, but 923 squeezed through the opening. Sally started toward the door first, but Blaise grabbed her arm, not wanting her to be the first to walk into danger. Sally looked back at him, and Blaise stepped past her and went through after 923.

He stepped through the door and into what was once the grand entryway of the tower. The ceilings were high and arched, and it looked like everything in there was made of marble. To his right was what was likely the main entrance, but the doors were boarded up to keep anyone out. There was still an opening at the top where some light from the Glow entered and reflected on the marble, but it was still mostly dark and filled with debris. Parts of the marble from the walls had broken off and were littering the floor. There seemed to be paper and trash floating around everywhere, and yet it was indeed one of the most beautiful places they'd ever seen. As Sally and Parker came through the door they too took note of it. They'd never quite seen anything glisten quite the way this room did.

"Nice, isn't it?" 923 said, taking note of their interest.

"I like it here. No one is supposed to be here, and usually no one is except for me."

Blaise ran his hand along the marble walls. They were smooth, cool, and strangely comforting. Sally started doing the same thing behind him, and they smiled at one another.

Parker kicked some broken marble across the floor, and stood in the middle of the room just looking around. 923 had moved into the back of the entryway. 923 watched Parker standing in the middle, and noticed that he was a little unsure of his surroundings.

"What's wrong? Don't you like it?"

"I just... I don't know," he responded. "I never thought this city could have something like this."

He looked down at the floor, stirred by the sight of the grand entryway and unsure how to comprehend it. 923 walked up to him, lifted his chin with her hand, and smiled at him. Parker felt a little awkward. They looked into each other's eyes for a moment before they each looked back down at the floor. They glanced up at each other again for a single moment and laughed a little.

Blaise and Sally looked on from afar, a little perplexed, at the two thin, weary humans who had just met and who now appeared to see mirrors of each other in their own sunken eyes. Sally rested her head on Blaise's shoulder, and they watched the exchange. 923 and Parker were lost in their own little world for a moment before 923 came down from the clouds and remembered what she was doing.

She looked over at Blaise and Sally part way across the room and said, "Let's keep moving," before heading back toward the back wall and opening another screeching door.

They followed her in and found themselves in a stairwell. It was darker in there, but there were still some small, red emergency lights that provided some visual on where they were going. They started up the stairs and went up several flights. They eventually came up to a large pile of rubble that had been that section of the stairs from just above. 923 climbed up onto it first and got her footing.

"This is a little tricky, but shouldn't be too much of a problem."

She took hold of a hanging rope that she had rigged up just for this purpose, and she started to climb it. Once she was just high enough, she was able to get her feet onto the stairs above and pull herself the rest of the way up. Parker followed next. He had a little trouble getting far enough up the rope to get his feet on the next set of stairs, but after a couple tries he succeeded.

"Alright, Sally, your turn," Blaise said.

"Okay," she responded, looking a little sheepish. She climbed onto the rubble being mindful of her ankle. She took the rope, but after several tries, she didn't feel like she could do it.

"Let's try this," Blaise said. He climbed on the rubble with her, knelt down, and interlocked his fingers.

"Let me hoist you up. Put your uninjured foot here, and then pull up on the rope."

She did just that and was up in no time. Blaise looked at the extra mud and dirt on his hands from Sally's shoe. He smirked, and then wiped them on his pants. Sally looked back down at him, smiled and said,

"Thanks!"

Blaise smirked again.

He got up the rope with little problem, and they all continued up the stairs for a while. They kept passing doors, and Blaise, Sally, and Parker kept hoping the next door would be their destination. Sally was moving the slowest, the stairs taking a significant toll on her ankle. But they waited for her, even if not so patiently. Regardless, her slow pace meant frequent rest breaks for everyone else. 923 finally stepped onto a landing ahead of them with a different kind of pep in her step.

"This better be it," Blaise thought. To everyone's delight, 923 did stop at the door on that landing and waited for the rest of the group to catch up. Once they were all gathered at

the door she said, "Well, let me officially welcome you to the towers," as she turned the knob and started to pull.

CHAPTER 4

Higher But Lower

923 opened the door to reveal what was behind it, and the first thing they felt was disappointment. They'd always heard grand stories about the towers, but they hadn't realized which of the three towers they were in. What they saw was not fun or exciting. It looked like the streets, just with a little higher elevation. The whole floor was made of little cubicles that looked to be either the same size or smaller than the room Blaise and Sally occupied in their building. For some sense of privacy, sheets were hung over the cubicles as roofs and doors. Other areas were simply divided entirely by sheets hanging over wires strung from wall to wall. It was dirty, and the smell was terrible.

923 looked around first before walking inside.

"We're clear. No Watchers," she said after a moment. "But let's move quickly and quietly."

The group went through the door at a hurried pace. They walked through a row of cubicles some of which had their sheet doors pulled back. Everyone there was wearing the same jumpsuit with a different number on the back. Blaise, Sally, and Parker glanced into some of the cubicles and saw some of them playing card games with others, some sleeping, and some staring at the ceiling. There weren't really any scowling faces. Most of the faces they saw were as blank as the Deep Darkness. Their eyes were just as empty too.

They kept moving through the rows, feeling exposed because they were the only ones not in jumpsuits. But no one said anything or seemed concerned. They came to a cubicle that looked like many others with a sheet for a door and a sheet draped on top of it as a ceiling. 923 pulled the curtain back and directed everyone inside. Sally went in first, then Blaise, then Parker, then 923. They all had to duck down to move around inside it. 923 turned on a single lamp she had, and they all sat down. The floor of the cubicle was covered in old blankets. In one corner was an old filing cabinet.

"It's not much, but it's mine," she said. She then crawled over to the filing cabinet and pulled out some jumpsuits.

"You'll need to put these on in case Watchers start to patrol."

Blaise, Sally, and Parker put on the jumpsuits over their clothes and zipped up the front zippers. Blaise tried to reach his head around to get a look at the back of it. "283" was blazoned on the back in large stenciled numbers. He felt an eerie chill. Once they were all uniformed, 923 spoke again.

"So. What do you want to do in the towers? Do you want to see the restaurants? The casinos? What is it that brings you here?"

Parker scratched his head. "Umm...what are those?"

"I always forget that street-dwellers don't know anything about restaurants and casinos. Well, a restaurant is where you go to get food, but instead of getting it yourself, someone brings it out to you. And a casino is where you bet money on games to see if you can get more money."

They stared at her for a second, still not understanding what she was talking about.

"Well, that's all fine," said Blaise, "but we're actually here for another reason."

Sally then interjected. "We need to warn the leader of the towers about something. How can we talk to whoever the leader is?"

923 let out a concerned laugh. "You don't just talk to Wilkins. Especially if you're wearing one of these jumpsuits."

Blaise scooted in a little closer. "Give us a chance. Point us in the right direction."

923 dropped her head and thought for a moment before speaking.

"Well, maybe, but regardless, Wilkins is probably sleeping now. Most of the Citizens went to sleep not long ago. That's why I was down on the streets. I sneak down there not long after everyone goes to bed. No one will be up for a while."

"So I guess we need to fill some time," Blaise said as he sat back against the cubicle wall thinking about what Mayor Max had said about attacking in one clock cycle.

"I have a game we can play," 923 said. "It's played a lot by us Attendants."

"Attendants?" Blaise asked. "We've been meaning to ask you about what that means."

923 crawled back over to the cabinet and pulled out a deck of cards.

"Well, that's what everyone in a jumpsuit is called."

She took the cards out of their pack.

"This is how the game works."

But Blaise didn't want her to change the topic.

"So...what's it like here...in the Towers?"

923 kept spouting off rules. It seemed like a very complicated game.

Sally was curious about Blaise's question too.

"We're very interested. We've always heard these wonderful stories about the..."

"Wonderful?" 923 said. "It's not wonderful. Not for us."

She put the cards down and looked at the floor. They were unsure whether she'd continue, but after a moment she sighed and lifted her head slightly, though she still looked down.

"Well, okay."

Blaise, Sally, and Parker leaned in.

"Where we are now is the third tower. It's where the Attendants dwell. That's everyone you see here in a jumpsuit with a number. We're forced to serve the Citizens. They dwell in the other two Towers and have all the fun and all the riches. They wear fancy clothes, go to their fancy dinners, and drink their fancy drinks, make us do all the work, and take all the beating."

That word sent a shock through Blaise, Sally, and Parker. "Beating?"

923 continued without pause.

"My job isn't too bad anymore. I work in the farms on the lower levels of this tower. That's a little better than working directly for a Citizen. It's been...a while...since I've been beaten."

No one dared to acknowledge the last part.

"Wait, farms? So the Towers do grow food?" said Parker.

"Yes. We use artificial light to grow grubs and a few plants. I hear that it's actually pretty tasty. Well, anyway, that's not too bad of a job. All you have to worry about is the Watchers. Kurtz almost never comes and oversees anything himself, but you better stay on your toes if he does."

"The Watchers?" asked Sally.

"They're the security force. They're not Citizens either, but they're treated a little better than us Attendants. You'll see one before long. They carry around bats and wear padded gear. That reminds me. Never ever speak to a Citizen or a Watcher without being spoken to first. That's a quick way to get in trouble. And don't look at anyone's eyes. That's a big no-no too. Just remember: It's Citizens first, then Watchers, and then Attendants. If someone is in a higher class, avoid those things."

Blaise shook his head in disgust. "Wow. So how is some-one's class decided?"

"Birth," 923 answered. "If your parents are Citizens, then you're a Citizen. If your parents are Attendants, you're an Attendant."

"What about your parents?" said Sally.

923 shook her head. "No. I don't have them. I was told that some street-dwellers traded me to the Towers for Bright when I was a baby....I'm no one's child."

There was a long pause before anyone spoke again. 923 let out a cleansing sigh and asked again.

"Do we want to play this game?"

Everyone agreed to at least try it. They attempted a few rounds, but it didn't really catch on. Whether that was because the game was uninteresting, or they were having more fun talking was unclear to them at the time. It was probably both. They smiled and laughed more than they likely ever had. Parker and 923 seemed to find a lot in common, not that the two of them really could have put it into words.

Parker and 923 got lost in conversation with each other and seemed to forget about Blaise and Sally. Blaise simply looked on. He'd never seen anyone, let alone Parker, interact with someone that way. Sally caught Blaise's attention as she yawned and rested her head on his shoulder. He contemplated things for a moment, wondering what it was that he was witnessing. He felt how weary he was, so he rested his head on Sally's.

Blaise woke up some time later. Sally was lying next to him, still asleep. He looked over and saw Parker laying on his back and 923 with her head on his chest. Waking up wasn't usually pleasant. No problem ever seemed resolved before falling asleep, and waking up meant facing them all over again.

Blaise stayed awake just lying there, thinking, but trying not to overthink; worrying, but trying not to over-worry. He was numb, however somewhat content; troubled, yet determined.

Parker and 923 stirred awake. They smiled at each other and laughed, wrapped in each other's arms. He looked over at Sally on her side facing him, still sleeping. He leaned over and touched his lips to hers. She opened her eyes slowly, blinking and squinting.

"Hi. What was that for?" she said with a smile on her face.

"Just...glad to have you around," Blaise responded sheepishly.

"Glad to have you around, too," Sally said, still smiling. Blaise just smirked and laid back on his back, staring up at the sheet covering the cubicle.

After a while when everyone was awake enough, 923 said, "Alright, are you all ready? I can lead you up to a point, but after that you're on your own."

"Okay, we better go," said Blaise.

They all filed out of the cubicle and stood up straight for the first time since getting into it. They stretched for a bit to loosen up.

"We have to go up one more level to get to a bridge," said 923.

They went through the rows of cubicles back to the door they had originally come in, went up one level, and came back out into a similar room of cubicles. But most of the Attendants were already out working. Before they went any further, 923 turned and looked at them sternly.

"Remember...Say nothing. Don't make eye contact with anyone. Look at the floor while you're walking."

They walked across the room through more cubicles to another door that led across a bridge to the middle tower. A Watcher was standing guard by it. 923 opened the door, and the four went through and across.

They got to the other side of the bridge, and she opened the door. On the other side was something beyond their wildest imaginings. It was a mall with different stores, restaurants, blinking neon lights, and fancy signs. The floor was packed to the walls with Citizens mingling through. They were loud, and they held their heads high, noses far in the sky. They were all wearing suits and dresses. To Blaise, Sally, and Parker, it was very strange clothing. Strange though it was, they couldn't help but think that the tower clothing was elegant and dignified, though still as torn and stained as their own.

With 923 leading, they shuffled through the throngs of Citizens all trying to avoid any contact or get in the way. They all took notice of a laughing, boisterous Citizen walking quickly toward them. He was looking around at all different things and speaking with others in the crowded mall. Blaise, Sally, and Parker tried to get out of his path, but before they could, someone called his name. He turned back, but kept moving forward and bumped right into Sally. The Citizen turned, looked at her, scowled, and spit on Sally's face.

"Stay out of the way, trash!"

Blaise grabbed her by the shoulders and kept her moving. Sally's eyes were wide, and she was shaking as she walked, the spit still on her face. They were all horrified at what had happened, but no one could do anything except keep walking.

They got to another stairwell on the other side of the floor and went through the door. As soon as it closed behind them, Sally broke down in tears. Blaise paused for a moment, understanding, but just hoping she'd get past it. After a moment though, he knew what he needed to do, and so he walked to her and hugged her as she cried. She cried even harder into his shoulder.

"Is this what it's like here, 923?"

"Yes. All the time," 923 responded. After a few more

moments, Sally pulled herself together. She lifted her head off of Blaise's chest and wiped her eyes.

"No point in crying more about it. Let's keep going," she said.

923 nodded in agreement. "We have to go up a few more flights to the casino. There's an elevator there that goes right to Wilkins' penthouse. Can I ask what you're trying to warn him about?"

Blaise hesitated for a moment and then confessed.

"The street-dwellers want to attack the towers. We think that's a bad idea, so we're trying to tell him to see if we can stop it."

923 shrugged. "Wow. But an attack wouldn't be so bad. The Citizens are too complacent up here. Maybe the street-dwellers attacking would let them know that it's not right to take advantage of them..."

923's words cut short and her head dropped.

"...And us."

Blaise was puzzled now too. Maybe it wasn't so clear what the best thing to do was. On the one hand, preventing conflict meant that everyone could go on existing the same way they always had. On the other hand though, comfort was its own form of violence; a slow, degenerative march away from any existence worth having.

"Well...better carry on," 923 said after finding the strength. They all moved silently, following her up the stairs. They didn't go up very many floors, but it felt like a heavy climb.

"Just a couple more, and we'll be there." 923 said while panting. A moment later she stopped walking and held her hand up to signal the others to do the same.

"Wait!"

Blaise, Sally, and Parker listened but heard nothing.

"What is it?" said Parker.

"Shh!...footsteps coming down."

The next door was up just one more flight. 923 started moving quickly up toward it, and the rest followed. They reached the landing and were met by a Watcher with a bat. 923 looked down. Blaise, Parker, and Sally forgot the rules 923 had laid out and looked right at him before realizing their mistake. Now all looking down, the Watcher spoke in an almost robotic, droning voice.

"Attendants, what is your destination?"

"Floor 57, Watcher." 923 pointed at the door.

"What are your assignments?"

"We're from agriculture. We were sent to make a delivery to the restaurant on this floor."

They could see just enough to know the Watcher looked around.

"Where is the delivery?"

"We already delivered it, but we were told to come back because there was a problem."

"What kind of problem?"

"A spoiled batch. We need to take it back."

"Are four Attendants required for this task?"

"It was several batches actually. We're all needed to carry it back."

"Acceptable. You are outside of your work zone though, so I'll need to verify your passes."

"Uh...Uh I think we must've left so quickly we forgot them."

"Forgot them?"

"Well yes, the restaurant was so upset, we were sent in a hurry."

"Every one of you forgot your passes?"

"Yes, I'm afraid so."

"Alright, I'll need to call backup to verify you."

The Watcher pulled his radio off of his waist and before he could activate it, 923 grabbed it and dropped it down the middle of the stairwell. The Watcher made a futile attempt to catch it but then slipped and fell down the stairs.

"Let's go!" said 923.

They went through the door and into another crowded mall area.

923 pointed toward a shop. "Over there!"

They walked quickly, trying not to draw any more attention. After some careful maneuvering through the crowd, they found themselves at the open entrance to a store. Upon walking in, the feeling of hustle gave way to a sense of quiet. There were only a few Citizens browsing the clothing racks, and some quiet music was playing.

There was an older, bearded man standing behind the counter with a tape measure around his neck. He looked up from his sewing machine. Blaise, Sally, and Parker tried to keep their heads down, but saw 923 nod at him. 923 kept leading them to the back of the store and then into the last changing room in a dark corner.

"Everybody just sit on the bench," 923 whispered. "Pull your feet up."

Wide-eyed and doing their best to breathe quietly, they all complied.

After several moments of silence, the tension began to subside. But before they could fully relax, the click of approaching shoes on the hard floor re-heightened the intensity. The clicks grew louder and louder until the feet in the shoes halted at the door. Worn, old leather dress shoes stood visible in the gap between the floor and the bottom of the door, toes pointed toward them.

923 slowly dropped her feet back to the ground. Everyone turned to her in silent shock. She stood up slowly and stepped toward the door.

"What is she doing?," Blaise thought. *"Is she betraying us? We shouldn't have trusted her!"*

923 turned the doorknob, still trying to be as quiet as possible. She opened it and stepped back. Standing in front of them was the man who'd stood behind the counter. He looked at each of them with a questioning look before looking at 923.

"Brought a whole crowd with you this time, didn't ya?"

"I'm afraid so, Carl," said 923.

"Well, it doesn't matter. I don't mind a challenge. I'll get you all sorted out."

Carl took his tape measure from around his neck and began measuring Blaise, Sally, and Parker.

"Lift your arms...turn around"

And all other things someone is usually told while being fitted.

"Okay. I think I've got just the things for each of you." Carl stepped out and closed the door.

He soon came back with four different clothes hangers.

"Here you are, 923. Your usual outfit," he said, handing

her a light, silky evening gown and a brunette wig. It had a big stain on the side, a few rips, and was very tattered around the hem. The wig was a little knotted but not so bad.

"I think this should suit you just fine," he said, giving Parker a collared shirt, slacks, and a vest with some flattened loafers that were worn in the sole. The seams in the shirt were a little pulled, the vest was missing buttons and the slacks had been patched.

Carl then turned to Sally.

"Now, I like this match, but let me know if you'd like something a little different."

He handed her a beautiful yet well-worn knee-length sundress. It had flowers on it. Something rarely seen, but what one might have come across in an old book.

Blaise stood waiting.

"You were a little difficult to find something for, but I think I found just the thing."

He gave Blaise a blue suit, a pair of brown shoes with a matching belt, and a gold bow tie. It smelled musty and the fabric was thin around the knees and elbows. The collar was frayed.

Carl stepped out with a smile and a nod.

"Thanks again!" 923 said. The rest echoed their appreciation.

Once he was out, they each put their clothes on over their jumpsuits, now thick with layers of their old clothes, their jumpsuits, and their new clothes. When they were all done they looked at themselves and each other in amazement.

"Wow. I never thought I might actually feel like a tower-dweller," Parker said. He puffed out his chest and stood up taller as he looked at his new self.

923 smiled at him, blushed, and then looked at the floor.

"You look the part."

"Well look at you! That dress. That wig. You look great with hair! ...I mean you look great without it too. I just meant..."

"It's okay. Thanks," she said, grinning at him.

Blaise had just been listening to their conversation when Sally caught his eye. She was looking at him just smiling a big smile. Blaise looked back at her and grinned wondering what she was smiling at.

"What?"

"Uh. Nothing. Just seeing you in that suit is kind of different and nice."

"Well uh...thanks, I guess."

Sally raised her eyebrow and gave him a look.

"O. I'm sorry! You look really nice too Sally!"

And she did. The dress accentuated her long, slender legs, and showed off just the right amount of her soft skin. "Is that all you have to say?"

Blaise shrugged. "What do you want me to say?"

Sally rolled her eyes but then smiled. "It's okay. Thank you."

Blaise and Sally's eyes turned back to 923 as she began to speak.

"Alright, this should make it easier to get where we need to go. Everybody ready?"

Parker interjected. "Well hold on. I know we need to do

what we came here to do, but we're in the Towers! We should have some fun!"

He looked at Blaise. Blaise looked at Sally. They all looked around at each other, and then they all turned back to Blaise.

"We really don't have much time to spare...." But by the looks on Parker and Sally's faces, he knew he wouldn't win. "Okay, fine, but let's be quick about it."

Parker let out an emphatic, "Yes!"

"But maybe we should split up two and two," Sally said. "We might attract less attention in smaller groups."

923 nodded in approval. "I like that idea. How about Parker and I go together, and you and Blaise go together?"

"That sounds like a plan," Sally said.

"Works for me," Blaise said. "Let's just plan to meet back here in this dressing room when we're done. Have fun. But don't take too long."

Parker was so excited that he was out the door and into the shop before Blaise could even finish talking. 923 left right behind him.

Blaise and Sally heard her say, "Wait up!" as the sound of their footsteps dwindled away.

Sally turned and smiled at Blaise.

"I have an idea of what we can do."

CHAPTER 5

Us

923 could hardly keep up with Parker. He was back out into the hustle and bustle of the mall before she could even get out of the changing area. She watched him look around the mall before looking back at her. He was standing up taller than ever before and with a big smile on his face.

"Come on! I see something fun over there!"

"I'm coming! I'm coming!"

Parker grabbed her hand and pulled her along.

They shuffled through the crowd until they came to a game room. It was dimly lit, but filled with little, blinking lights, and a lot of different funny noises. Bells were dinging. There was something that sounded like a siren.

"This?" 923 said. "This is just an arcade. Most of the games aren't even fun."

Parker didn't say anything. 923 looked at him and could see the wonder on his face. She could see the flashing lights glitter in his wide eyes. Drool started to form at the corner of his mouth.

Her attitude changed. She couldn't help but smile at him.

"Okay, let's go!" she said.

She marched into the arcade with Parker in tow.

Parker walked over to a machine. "What is this?"

"It's a pinball machine," said 923. "You have to pull this back."

She reached in front of him to show him, but his eyes were locked on her.

923 blushed, smiled, and looked away, but continued her demonstration. She released the ball launch and they both watched as the ball soared freely up and into the machine. It started bouncing haphazardly on all of the different things inside as it came back toward them.

"Okay. Now you have to use the paddle buttons on either side to keep from losing the ball."

Parker tried to find what buttons 923 was talking about, but the ball had already dropped.

"Darn!"

"It's okay. Try it again."

Parker found the buttons and then launched another ball. He tried it a few times with some success and a little more frustration.

"I've got an idea," 923 said. "You control that paddle and I'll control this paddle. Let's see how well we can do."

"Okay!"

"Launch another one!" she said.

Parker pulled the ball launcher back and let it fly.

"Watch out, 923! It's coming to your paddle!"

"O no!"

The ball rolled off of 923's paddle and down out of play.

"That was fun. Let's keep trying that," said Parker.

They were soon lost in their game and lost in each other, forgetting everything else around them. The stress and weight of their existence melted away revealing a capability for playfulness and laughter that neither had ever experienced. It was addicting.

At the forefront of Parker's mind was 923's smiling face, her endearing timidity, and his growing care for her. In the back of his mind he thought about how much better this moment was than using Bright. Bright gave him an empty luminescence, but 923 was pure light standing in contrast to the dark background of their difficult and inescapable pasts and futures. And like light does, it drove out that darkness and made way for the beautiful present.

What surprised Parker most about her was that despite the horrors of her existence, she still found ways not to be miserable. This, he realized, was the very thing that drew him to her the most. He shrunk at this thought, knowing full well that such a human as he had no business with such a human as her.

After a time, Parker's eyes drifted from the pinball machine and onto 923. She was still focused on the game.

"Parker! Parker! Hit your paddle! We're about to lose the ball!"

He said nothing. He just kept looking at her, taking her in.

"O no!"

The machine let out a series of descending pitches.

"Why didn't you hit your paddle?" she said before looking in his direction.

She looked up to see him looking back at her. Their eyes locked for a moment. 923 could feel her chest tighten as she tried the hardest she ever had to look into another's eyes. But she turned away anyway.

Her thoughts tortured her. *"Why can't I do it?"*

She became increasingly angry at herself as she stared at the floor. She stamped her foot in frustration. That only made her more angry at herself. Here she was, too shy and damaged to be anything but worthless to anyone else. Or so she thought. And there he was, so tender and caring. Why should anyone like him be with someone like her?

Tears came down her face.

"I have to get out of here," she thought. And at the moment that she began to lift her foot to take a step, 923 felt something on her chin. Parker's warm, yet dirty and calloused hand, lifted it. Tears kept coming down her face, but Parker's expression didn't change. She could see the adoration in his eyes, the concern in his brow, and though only in hindsight, she'd come to think of him in that moment as having an aura shining around him.

Parker looked at the broken individual standing in front of him. He could sense her pain, shame, and unspeakable wounds. The tears on her face were the price he was more than willing to pay if it meant he could be the one she smiled at.

"But who am I to deserve her?" he thought. *"I'm just a thief and a coward, addicted to Bright. She'd hate me if she really knew about me."*

Tears started forming in his eyes too. He clenched his other fist and looked down. He too was about to step away, but before he could do anything her arms surrounded him with the tightest hug he had ever received. He was a little surprised at first, but then he felt relieved. The tension ran out of his shoulders, and he hugged her back. She rested her head on his chest. He rested his head on her head. They stayed like that for a long time, oblivious to the rest of the city and what they thought.

Parker then had an idea. He lifted his head and looked at her. She looked back at him, her mouth quivering, but this time her eyes locked on his.

"You need a name. 923 isn't a name."

Her eyes lit up, and a big smile came across her face.

"Name? For...for an Attendant? The Citizens wouldn't..."

"The Citizens don't need to know. Even if the name is just between us, you need a name. You're too much to be a number."

She lit up and hugged him more tightly than before, nearly knocking him over. Then she looked at him again,

"Okay. So...wha...what should my name be?"

"You don't want to pick it?"

"Okay, I guess I'll try. Umm...I like Sally. She's really nice. I could be Sally too."

Parked chuckled. "No, no, no. Something unique."

923 looked down, thinking. "If I'd had parents they would've named me. But I don't and they didn't. Names are given. They're given by the ones..." then she looked back up at Parker, "or *one* who cares the most."

She smiled a huge smile. "You should name me."

"Oh... Okay," he said, a little abashed. "I'll give it a shot."

He stood there thinking for an awkward while. *"Well...how about...no...or maybe..."*

"I've got it!" He said it confidently, though he was unsure that she would like it. "Nine is the first number in 923. So how about...Nina?"

She nodded, looking a little unsure. She looked to the side, repeating it over and over. "Nina...Nina...Nina..."

Parker was now certain that she hated it.

But then she looked at him, smiling again with tears in her eyes.

"I have a name. It's Nina. And you gave it to me."

***

"What do you want to do?"

Sally smiled a big smile, then blushed. "I don't know. Nevermind. Maybe it's silly."

"No, really. What do you want to do?"

"It's fine. You don't look like you want to."

"No, I do! Tell me."

"Well, okay. I was thinking... that...we should...have a fancy dinner at a tower restaurant like 923 was telling us about."

Blaise weighed the idea for a moment, and the more he thought about it, the more he liked it.

"Okay! Let's do it!"

Sally's face lit up into a huge smile. "This'll be so much fun!"

They left the changing room and started walking through the store.

Blaise felt a sense of levity come over him.

"Maybe it is time for some fun," he thought. He stood up tall, puffed out his chest, and offered his arm to his lady.

She gladly took it, and the two started walking down the mall looking for just the right place to eat. Blaise felt like a King at that moment, and Sally like a Queen. They each pushed their troubles below the surface and marched up and out, committing more and more to their charade with each passing step.

Holding their chins high, they tried to walk in a dignified way, gliding through the mall with grace and poise, oblivious to how over-exaggerated their efforts were.

"Where should we dine, my lady?"

"Excellent question, kind sir."

Sally looked around and spotted a place that appeared to be serving plates. It had script lettering that neither of them could have read even if they knew how, and a man in a tuxedo was standing at the door.

"That's where!" Sally said.

Blaise gave her a stately and affirming nod, and escorted her over to and right past the man in the tuxedo. They started looking around for a table, wondering which one to pick when the man in the tuxedo tapped Blaise on the shoulder.

"Excuse me, sir, madam. Would you like to be placed on the seating list?"

"Uh...uh yes please," Blaise said.

"Of course. It shouldn't be a long wait."

"Oh. Okay. Sorry about that," Sally said as they walked back to the front of the restaurant and sat on a bench just outside.

"We didn't exactly think this through, did we?" Sally said through a smile.

"Yeah, not exactly," Blaise grinned. "Let's try not to be so obvious that we don't belong here."

Sally laughed a little, and so did he. She rested her head on his shoulder and they just sat there for a while, watching tower-dwellers go by.

"Look at that guy, Blaise. He looks important. Other tower-dwellers are moving out of his way."

"I'm not sure if they're moving out of his way because he's important, or because he can't see where he's going because his nose is so far in the air."

Sally smiled. "I think you might be right. And the lady trailing behind can hardly keep up."

"By the look on her face, she's trying to keep up appearances. She's not happy," Blaise said.

Sally's smile faded as she looked at the woman. "Yeah, she has a kind of sad smile, doesn't she?"

That pair disappeared into the crowd, and soon two older boys walked by laughing and talking. Blaise and Sally heard a few bits of their conversation before they too disappeared into the crowd.

"Who's that girl you were with the other day?"

"Which one?"

"What do you mean which one?"

"I'm a little more sly than I let on I guess."

"I saw you at the casino with whoever this is."

"O, her? She's kind of annoying."

"She's easy on the eyes though."

"Well she is that. That's why I haven't dropped her yet."

"You're awful. I'd do the same thing though."

After the boys were out of sight, a scruffy, tired-looking man in a mismatched suit came stumbling toward them. He was hunched over and could barely walk. There was a bottle in one hand and he was holding out his other to keep what was left of his balance. Blaise and Sally's eyes widened as he got closer and closer to them. The man almost fell on top of them before he too got wide-eyed and realized what he was about to do.

"oooo....hic...sorryyy," he said as he stumbled off in another direction.

"That was close," Sally said with a laugh.

"I did not want to have to pick him up off of the floor," Blaise said.

"Looks like someone else got that privilege." She pointed over to a couple of Watchers lifting him by both arms and carrying him off.

As they were trying to see where he was being dragged, the man in the tuxedo stepped in front of them.

"Your table is ready. If you would please follow me."

Blaise and Sally stood up and followed him back inside the restaurant. There were a number of tables already occupied by Citizens. Blaise and Sally tried to catch glimpses of what was on their plates, narrowly looking down their noses trying not to be too obvious.

The man in the tuxedo stopped at a small table for two. Blaise and Sally were amazed by it. It was draped with a formerly white, but now brown-tinged tablecloth. Two mismatched plates sat on either side of the table. Both were quite scratched, and one even had a large chip out of it. Tarnished and bent silverware lay just beside the plates.

"Your table," said the man in the tuxedo.

"Uh...thanks," Blaise said as the man in the tuxedo walked back to the front.

Blaise and Sally took their seats. Each chair wobbled and creaked a little bit, but was otherwise comfortable. They tried to hide their laughs as they peered at each other by the light of the candle on their table.

"I can't believe we're doing this," Sally said. "We'll be found out for sure."

Blaise smiled back. "Let's play it cool, and we'll be okay. Maybe we can look around and copy what others are doing."

"That works."

They watched as other tuxedoed tower-dwellers moved around talking to those seated at tables. The tuxedoed tower-dwellers would go through a door and come back out with trays of food to bring to different tables. The tuxedo men were taking down notes on notepads and the table-sitters would smile at some of them and frown, or even yell, at others. It was hard to take everything in and figure out what to do. They both felt a growing sense of confusion and disorientation as one of the tuxedoed tower-dwellers stepped up to their table.

"Hello sir, madam. I will be your server. Is this your breakfast, lunch, or dinner?"

Blaise gulped. "Uh...um...uh...lunch...I guess..."

"Excellent. We're serving a wonderful toasted grub sandwich that comes with a side of baked mushroom."

"Um, sure. That sounds okay. What about you, Sally?"

"I think I'll get that too."

"Right away," said the tuxedoed man as he walked off.

Blaise and Sally looked at each other and laughed.

"Did I sound stupid?" Blaise said. "I feel like I sounded stupid."

Sally just laughed some more.

Blaise smiled. "Okay. Well look. I don't know what I'm doing."

"Clearly," Sally snickered.

There was then a long pause. Blaise and Sally found themselves unexpectedly speechless in each other's presence. They each looked around the restaurant at whatever they could focus on, making the occasional glance at the other. There were a few grunts and sighs but no words until Sally finally gained the courage to speak.

"Do you remember when we first met?"

Blaise nodded. "Yeah. Seems like so long ago now."

"Feels like it was only a little while ago too."

"A little bit of both, I guess."

Blaise saw a contemplative look on Sally's face. She looked both a little bit happy and a little bit sad.

"I...I...admired your determination. Of all those who'd given up on the Glow, you still stood on the overlook. You had such enthusiasm. I was drawn to you because of it."

"Yeah. I was a little crazy back then. Rowing out into the water, thinking I'd actually get somewhere."

Sally laughed a little. "It seemed silly to me at first, but after a while I started to believe because you did." She looked up at Blaise's face. "I remember when I first walked up to you while you were working on that boat. You were so happy to talk to someone about the Glow and about trying to get to it."

Blaise smiled. "You were around from then on. I remember I got mad one time because you messed up one of the patches I'd done on the boat."

Sally laughed. "Oh yeah. I forgot about that."

"But that was okay. It was nice to have someone to talk to."

Sally got quiet for a moment and stared off into the restaurant. "Do you remember our first kiss?"

"Of course," Blaise said. "I remember feeling a little awkward just sitting on the beach together. Neither of us were saying anything, and I was trying to work up the nerve to go for it."

Sally blushed. "But I was just sitting there hoping you would."

"Well I know that now," Blaise said with a smile.

"When we kissed, I knew we weren't going to be apart after that," Sally said.

"And we haven't been," Blaise said.

Sally then got a big smile on her face. "Not long after that we got our room. We'd just sit there and hold each other in that rickety bed for I don't even know how long."

"That was nice," Blaise said. "We'd fight and make-up and fight and make-up over and over again."

"True. But neither of us ever went anywhere, did we?"

"No. We sure didn't."

Another moment of silence passed before Sally spoke again. "What's your favorite memory of us?"

"Um...well...I don't know."

"Come on, you have to have something."

Blaise sat thinking for an awkward amount of time. "I think I know. I liked when we would walk up and down the street just to talk and hold hands. We did that pretty often for a while. That's a nice memory."

Blaise felt satisfied by Sally's soft smile. "I liked that too. That was nice."

"Anything else?" Sally asked.

"I don't know. Not really."

Blaise shifted in his chair. "What...um...is your favorite memory?"

Sally blushed, smiled, and laughed a little. She then let out a cleansing sigh.

"Where do I begin?" She sat back in her chair. "I've just liked every time I've seen you smile, every time you've laughed. It's always made me feel like I've gotten to the Glow when you've hugged me tightly. I like to think about the times we just sat on the beach without any thought of doing anything else except being together. Or the times we'd run down to the Arena and just play jokes on everyone there."

Blaise smiled. "I forgot about that."

Sally smiled back and continued. "One time you dared me to walk up to someone random and pretend to bump into them. It was so dumb, but we thought it was so funny. We laughed and laughed so much all the way back to the room that we could hardly walk. I remember the look on that one guy's face. He started coming after us until we managed to lose him in the crowd."

Sally's smile faded as she thought. "It's not always been easy. There was the time we were struggling to find food and you were getting more and more stressed the hungrier we got. We finally found a can of beans, and we were so excited. But when you went to pour it into the pot, half of the beans fell into the fire." She shook her head and looked tearful.

"You just broke down sobbing, and all I could do was stand there and hug you. We just cried together for a while and then ate our quarter can of beans each."

Her smile came back. "It's been fun. It's been tough. But I wouldn't have it any other way."

Blaise just smiled back at her and didn't say anything.

A tuxedo man came with their plates of food and set them down in front of them.

"Voila! Enjoy your meal." He walked off back into the kitchen.

"Wow! This looks very tasty," Blaise said. He picked up his fork and started to eat his grubs. Sally picked up her fork, but just watched Blaise for a moment. She then looked at her plate and ate a few bites. Blaise saw her keep looking back at him, but he tried to pretend that he didn't see her. He saw her mouth open a little like she was about to say something. She then closed it and kept eating. Before long he saw her put down her fork and look right at him.

"But you've been distant lately, Blaise."

He stopped eating and looked up at Sally's teary eyes.

"You...you don't look at me the same way you used to. You're different."

Blaise struggled to find words. "I...I don't understand. I'm the same me I've always been."

"No.... You've faded. Yeah, you still look at the Glow, but you're angry at it. It's not the same wonder you once had. And yeah, you look at me, but you gaze right through me like I'm not even there."

"I've never treated you badly or said I didn't want to be around you. What are you talking about?"

Sally sighed and looked back down at her plate. A tear formed on her cheek.

"Nevermind. It's okay. Let's just enjoy our food."

Blaise stared down at his plate lost in his thoughts. *What just happened?* Any words he thought to say seemed inadequate. *"This was supposed to be fun,"* he thought. *"Now it's all ruined, and I don't even know why. Here's this beautiful girl in front of me, and apparently I don't even know how to care for her."*

The tuxedoed man walked back toward the table with a piece of paper in his hand. Blaise felt a little relief that this awkward moment might end. He placed the piece of paper face down on the table.

"I hope all has been to your pleasure. Here is your bill." He then walked off to another table.

Blaise looked at Sally. "Uh...bill?"

"Don't look at me," Sally said. "I don't know."

Blaise waved over to the tuxedoed man who was still talking to the other table. He gestured that he would be over soon. After another moment, he came back.

"Yes, sir?"

"Um...yes," Blaise said. "I can't see well, and I forgot my glasses. Could you tell me what the bill says?"

"O, yes, of course, sir." He picked it up off of the table and read it. "Fifty-two silver coins to be paid."

"O...okay. Yes. Thank you," Blaise said before the tuxedoed man walked away.

"Uh...Blaise...we don't have fifty-two silver coins."

"I know."

"What should we do?"

Blaise thought for a moment and saw no other alternatives. "Maybe we should just get up and leave."

"He's facing away from us right now. This may be our chance," Sally said.

They quickly stood up from their chairs and moved quickly to the exit, but not too quickly so as to avoid drawing attention. With each passing step, they felt more and more anxious to get away.

"Only a few more steps to the exit," Blaise thought. That's when he heard a loud "Stop them!" from back in the restaurant.

Blaise and Sally didn't look back. They ran out and into the crowd.

***

With every creak and ding of the dark, old, and yet, somehow, still climbing, elevator, the man in it grew more and more nervous. It would have been a relief to him if it had broken down and trapped him inside. But despite his wishes, it just kept moving. The two Watchers standing on either side of him didn't help him feel any better.

The elevator made screeching noises that sounded like metal grinding against metal. One screech continued for so long that it started to sound like a scream. Then there was silence for a moment or two. That helped him relax just enough so that the loud, piercing screech that followed was even more frightening. Despite his startled jump, the Watchers didn't move. Their eyes stayed straight ahead, their bats still held across their chests.

There was dried blood on the ends of a few of the nails. Seeing this, he gulped and turned back toward the door. The sweat was pooling on his hands as he knew they were reaching the top. The mechanism to indicate what floor they were on was broken, but it had been about as much time as he'd remembered it taking the last time he was there.

He remembered the time long before. It had all been conniving smiles and the putrid, yet delightful camaraderie of scoundrels.

"I'm sure we can keep them in check working together," the now fearful man had said to his conspirator, glad then to have been given an approving smirk. The two had shaken hands, shared a drink, and got back to business. He remembered feeling dreadfully proud and horribly unconquerable.

But now he felt more like a frightened child. The elevator began to slow, so he closed his eyes and took a slow, deep breath. It came to a stop and let out a weak sigh. The doors squealed open. The man could see Ambrose standing and looking out the window in his usual posture, a pitch black silhouette against the distant Glow. Rubbing his eyes and looking harder, it seemed as though there was even the faintest dark aura surrounding him.

Not realizing that he had stopped walking, one of the Watchers prodded him in the back with the butt of their bat. He scowled but knew better than to argue. The other Watcher made a motion toward the old, satin couch. He walked over to it and sat down slowly, keeping his eyes on Ambrose who stayed fixed at the window. The Watchers moved to a position behind the couch.

The record player was projecting dark and ominous music that was heavy with stringed instruments. It was entertaining for the man even if it was also a little frightening.

"Not a....not a bad piece of music, eh ol' Ambrose? What is it?"

Ambrose dropped his head but did nothing else.

"What are those instruments you think? I once heard of something called a violin. I think there might be a few in this."

Ambrose turned his head and shoulders and glared at the man before shaking his head and turning back.

The man looked around while tapping his fingers on the arm rest. The turning record caught his eye for a moment, and when he looked back, Ambrose was standing in the same spot but now facing him.

In a voice attempting calm, Ambrose spoke.

"What...happened...with the plans?"

"Uh...uh...I did what you commanded, didn't I Ambrose? It's not my fault that hardly anyone actually showed up."

Dr. Ambrose stared at his guest as he shifted nervously on the old, satin couch.

"What am I supposed to do? You've got them too hooked on Bright to be of any use."

Ambrose's fist tightened as his other hand held it behind his back.

"How many showed up?" he asked through gritted teeth.

"I didn't count exactly. Maybe twenty-five."

Ambrose hung his head and then walked to stand in front of the couch. The man looked up at the towering figure who stood ominously close. Even the shadow across his face couldn't hide his burning eyes.

He shifted uncomfortably on the couch as he watched the rage build on Ambrose's face.

"You and your ridiculous 'Mayorship'!" he yelled through

gritted teeth, his spit hitting him in the face. "What use are you!? I knew I shouldn't have trusted garbage to take out garbage!"

Those words stung Mayor Max but, to his great relief, Ambrose started to pace away toward the record player. Mayor Max flinched because he thought Ambrose may simply throw it off of the end table at him, but instead he lifted the needle off and placed it back in its spot.

The silence now added to Mayor Max's discomfort, and so he clamored to find whatever words he could.

"I mean, we can try again. Maybe I could promise anyone who joins the offensive more Bright if you supply it. Or how about just food? Or...or...withhold food! That's it! They'll get so hungry they'll have to fight."

Ambrose turned back with an even nastier glare. Mayor Max gulped and tried to sink into the couch.

"O yes, stop sending food just so you can get richer and fatter by selling your own."

Max's heart sank, and his face went pale. Ambrose noticed this and took advantage of it, coming right back up to him. Ambrose got right in his face.

"That's right. I know exactly what you've been doing in direct defiance of my orders."

"Ambrose, Ambrose. Please...." but he tapered off, looked down, and closed his eyes.

Then, sensing that Ambrose had stood up and moved away, Max opened his eyes and looked up at Ambrose just in time to see him nod at a Watcher.

"Wait! No! Ambrose! I'll make this right!"

As he was pleading, everything went dark. A black bag was

now over his head. He felt the Watchers grab him by the arms and he was then pulled over the back of the couch.

"We can work this out Ambrose! Please, stop them!"

He sagged his weight and dragged his feet to try and delay, but they only grabbed his arms more tightly and pulled him back toward the elevator.

Ambrose now stood at the window again scouring at the Glow. The elevator bell sounded its dissonant twang. As the door closed, Mayor Max heard him speak from across the room.

"Consider our arrangement terminated. Watchers...send him back to the streets...as quickly as possible."

Mayor Max felt relieved as he was dragged onto the elevator.

"Okay, back to the streets then, I suppose," he thought. He stood back on his feet feeling a bit more confident.

"But then why the black bag?"

His heart sank all over again as he felt the elevator go up instead of down.

CHAPTER 6

Highest or Lowest

"Where could they be?" Sally was exasperated. Blaise felt the same way, but was just trying to stay focused as best he could. They'd already checked for them at the clothing store, but it was all locked up, and Carl had left.

They each swung their heads around to look, but it was difficult through all the flashing lights and throngs of Citizens. What they did see, however, were Watchers doing the same looking for them.

After much irritation, Sally saw them.

"There!"

Blaise turned to look. Through a crowd of tower-dwellers playing the arcade games, he saw them. They were leaning on the pinball machine, looking into each other's eyes, smiling, laughing, and otherwise oblivious to everything else around them. Blaise was immediately irritated and, though he didn't admit to himself, envious.

He clenched his fist and stomped his way over to them,

Sally floating gently behind. He was ready to rant and rave as soon as he got to them.

"Let's go! We don't have time to stand around!" was what he thought he'd yell.

But as he got nearer, all that anger faded away as he was taken in again by the odd and other-wordly, yet calm and comfortable, sight he had first seen in the cubicle.

Parker took his time and then slowly looked up at Blaise.

"Hey...Blaise...," he said before looking back at 923.

And not at all in the way he had planned to say it, but rather calmly and quietly, Blaise said, "Let's go. We don't have time to stand around."

"What's the matter?" said Parker, still looking at 923.

Blaise put his hand on his shoulder. "Watchers are coming and...I'm not sure, but I think we may run out of time before the street-dwellers attack."

Parker shrugged and kept his eyes locked on 923.

"Come on. We really need to go."

923 sighed. "He's right, Parker. We ought to get out of here if there are Watchers."

"Okay, *Nina*," Parker said, putting emphasis on her new name but otherwise with very little urgency.

She leaned over and put her head on Parker's chest.

"Nina?" said Sally.

"That's my name now." Her smile got wide and her eyes a little teary, but only for a moment before the former faded and the latter widened.

"The door," she whispered.

Two Watchers were standing at it looking into the arcade.

"Let's move into the back," Nina said under her breath.

The four kept calm as best they could and started walking farther into the arcade. They made it to the very back past a few busted machines and went into a dark alcove. Blaise glanced around the corner and saw the Watchers continuing in, stopping to check each tower-dweller.

"What now?" Sally asked.

"I don't know," Blaise responded. "923...I mean...Nina. Do you have any ideas?"

She stood a little taller at hearing her name but then shook her head. "All we can do is wait."

"Let's hope they just turn back," said Parker.

Blaise peered around again. They were on the last tower-dweller before the busted machines.

"Please turn back. Please turn back," Blaise repeated in his head.

Knowing now that if he looked he'd most certainly be seen, he just stayed and waited.

"Please turn back. Please turn back." But their footsteps got closer and Blaise could sense they were just around the corner.

"Watchers! Watchers!," they heard from near the entrance. "A boy just took coins from the token machine! Yes! That way. He went out of the arcade and down that stairwell!"

The Watchers turned and went.

Despite knowing that they were gone, Blaise, Sally, Nina, and Parker stayed quiet for a little longer just to be sure. Then they were all startled by someone else coming around the corner. The figure wasn't in Watcher gear, but his face was in a shadow.

"I thought I recognized those clothes. Nobody stitches them up like me."

Carl stepped up into a ray of light so they could see him, and they all slumped to the floor in relief.

"We're sure glad to see you," Nina said, picking herself back up.

"Anything for you, my dear. But you better get out of here while you have a chance."

They all stood up and left. Getting back to the entrance of the arcade, Carl looked around.

"I don't see any Watchers. I think you're okay for now, but don't stay out in the open."

And before they could even thank him or say farewell, Carl trotted off.

"Let's get to the casino," Nina said.

They moved through the crowd to the stairwell door and climbed a few more flights before coming to another door.

"Is this it?" Blaise asked. Nina turned to him and smirked.

"This is the casino. It takes up the whole floor, and it's the biggest party in the whole city."

She opened the door, and they were hit with a wall of sound. Lights were flashing. Bells were dinging. Buzzers were ringing. The Citizens there were talking, laughing, drinking, and smoking. Some were pulling levers on the old, busted slot machines that still worked. Others were playing cards, and others were standing around the bar. They thought they'd seen as loud and vibrant a place as they ever could in the shopping area, but the casino outdid it easily.

But as they started walking in, they quickly noticed something else. Yes, many were laughing and smiling, and throwing their hands up in excitement, but when they looked closely they could see just as many frustrated, sad, and lonely faces. One tower-dweller sat at a slot machine with his head resting on it. His eyes were open, just blankly looking down, tears dropping onto the machine.

Another man sat at the bar right next to a clique of laughing tower-dwellers. He too sat with an empty stare, hunched over and blank. Every so often one tower-dweller in the rowdy group next to him would unknowingly bump into him with his back. The man hardly reacted to it. He just sat there in the shadow of their delight.

They began walking through the casino, shuffling through Citizens sideways for most of the way. Before long they came to a more secluded area in a corner behind a row of machines far enough away that no one was using them. Nina looked around and then ducked, directing everyone else to do the same.

"Do you see that elevator a few rows over?"

They each stood up just enough to see over the machines and see the elevator door she was referring to.

"That's the elevator to Wilkins' penthouse. You need a key to use it." She pulled that key out of her pocket.

"I used to be Wilkins' own Attendant...before he got angry with me." She paused. "Take it. It's the only way you're going to get to him." Sally reached out and took the key.

"Go," Nina said, both sternly and reluctantly.

"You're not coming?" Parker said.

"I can't," she said as tears started coming down her face. "If I go, he'll kill me, or worse. I'm sure of it."

He hugged Nina tightly. They kissed.

"Just Go." Tears were streaming down her face. They put their foreheads together, both crying.

"Go!" she said again but a little too loud, as if she were trying to rip off a bandage.

Blaise, Sally, and Parker stood up from behind the machines and went around the corner and several rows over to the elevator. They frantically pushed the up button until the doors grinded open, the elevator showing no sign of urgency. Blaise and Sally stepped on. Parker hesitated. He looked back over to where they had been crouched and saw Nina's face peeking around the corner of the machines. All he could bear to do was nod slightly, look away, and walk in.

Sally inserted the key and hit the button for the penthouse. They looked around at each other, concerned. This is why they'd gone on this journey, but now that they were so close, they were having second thoughts. But for better or worse, they were going to talk to Wilkins, the leader of the towers.

The elevator crept up, making frequent screeching noises. It kept going and going. They wanted to get to the top, but they were also terrified of what they'd encounter. Was Wilkins really as horrifying as they were imagining? Would they meet the same fate that Nina feared? Tensions rose in each of them as they moved farther and farther up the tower.

Finally and unfortunately, the elevator began to slow down and screech to a halt. They all felt a twist in their stomachs as the doors opened. As more of the room was revealed they saw what few ever did: the quarters of the self-proclaimed overlord of the dark city. They saw the table with the three chairs around it, the ornate decorations and beautiful windows all around the room.

But they also saw something they could not have expected. They saw a figure in a black and hooded cloak wielding a sword in its right hand. The figure had its back to them, looking out the window. They slowly stepped out into the room. The figure didn't seem to take notice at first. While Blaise was focused on it, Sally jumped toward Blaise and clung to his arm. Blaise looked at Sally whose face had turned pale as she looked at something on the floor. Blaise looked past Sally and saw a dead Watcher; face down in a pool of his own blood, weapon still in hand. Blaise's eyes got wide.

He looked back toward the cloaked figure, but this time it had turned toward them. The figure filled the room with a powerful sense of emptiness. He could see that the figure was wearing a black mask as horrifying as the Deep Darkness. The figure's sword was red with blood. It then turned back toward the window, and viciously swung at it with its sword, shattering it into countless pieces. The air pressure changed drastically, causing a heavy wind inside the room. Blaise, Sally, and Parker tried to stand their ground. The dark figure sheathed the sword, spread its arms, and dove out of the building.

Before long, the air pressure balanced out. They gathered themselves for a moment, as it remained quiet in the room. They could tell they were now alone. Soon after, they saw the tall backs of two chairs around the table with arms resting on their armrests. Neither seemed to move. Blaise moved slowly forward, signaling to Sally and Parker to stay back. He got to the backs of the chairs and crept around to get a glimpse of who was on the other side. He saw sitting in each chair two faces staring back at him with their throats slit. He looked back over at Sally and Parker.

"Dead."

Sally came over next to Blaise and covered her mouth in shock. "Do...do you...do you think one of them is Wilkins?"

"Probably."

Parker stayed as far away as possible. "Wh...what was that cloaked thing?"

Blaise shook his head. "No idea."

"Maybe we should look around," said Sally.

Upon hearing her say that, Blaise's eyes got wide with an idea. "Yes...yes. Let's look around."

He saw some large bookshelves over on one side filled with different folders and files and made his way over to them. Parker stayed glued to his spot and Sally went looking around at other things.

Muttering to himself the only word he could read, he pulled numerous files looking to see if it was on any of them.

After some time looking, he saw a marker with a "G" on it. He moved to that section and pulled each of the files in it until he found a folder with "Glow" on the front of it among a few other words. It was thick with paper–thicker than almost any other file. And as much as Blaise wanted to take the whole thing with him, he knew he couldn't. He took the front page out and folded it up. He safely tucked it in the pocket of his old pants, under both his suit and jumpsuit.

Parker still didn't look like he'd moved. His face was white, and he was just standing and staring.

Sally was over on the other side of the penthouse.

"Blaise, come see this stuff."

He walked over to see what she was looking at. There were cabinets full of very ornate plates, silverware, jewelry, and other valuables. All were tarnished and dirty, but still nicer than they'd ever seen.

Sally shook her head. "Wilkins thought he was so rich, but I wouldn't feel comfortable being here."

She looked at Blaise with a little smile. "I like what we have."

Before Blaise could respond, she kept walking, looking at all of Wilkins' things.

Then came a grim voice through the shadows in the outer edges of the penthouse that struck fear back into them.

"What have you done?"

Dr. Ambrose stepped from the shadows, hands clasped behind his back, and walked over to the dead men in the chairs. He whipped his head toward Blaise.

"Explain yourself!"

"We...we...didn't," Blaise responded.

Ambrose walked toward him. Blaise was frozen in place, and Ambrose was now uncomfortably close, causing Blaise to take one step back. Ambrose just looked at him with a quizzical look. Blaise saw him squint as if noticing something. Ambrose reached out with his finger and pulled down the collar of his dress shirt revealing just enough of the Attendant jumpsuit. Then came a frightening grin of approval.

Dr. Ambrose went over to the table and touched his hand to the bottom of it, appearing to press a button. He grinned as he took his normal seat. As Blaise stood wide-eyed and struggling to comprehend the situation, Watchers rushed in from every entrance to the room. They had nowhere to go.

"Take these murderers into custody," Ambrose barked at the Watchers. Blaise looked toward Sally and Parker. Watchers quickly surrounded them all. Sally turned to Blaise, and his heart sank at seeing the look of desperation in her eyes. But she too saw the desperation in his–each of them wishing they could save the other–each knowing they were helpless to do so. Parker tried to struggle with the Watchers as they tried to get him on the ground and get his hands behind his back. Something blunt hit Blaise in the back of his legs, forcing him to his knees. A foot on his back pushed him the rest of the way to the ground. As his face was pressed against the floor, he looked back toward Sally and saw that she was in the same position on the ground looking back at him. He saw one of the Watchers near Sally pull out a black bag. The Watcher put the black bag over Sally's head, and now unable to see Sally's face, it felt as though the wind had been knocked out of him. As he laid there fearing that he may never see her face again, a bag went over his head too, and everything went black.

The next thing Blaise knew, there was a sharp pain lingering in the back of his head. He was very disoriented and trying to regain his bearings. The bag was still over his head, but from what he could tell, he was tied to a chair and probably outside. It was windy, but otherwise quiet.

As he was still trying to regain his composure, the bag was suddenly pulled off of his head. His eyes were immediately met by a bright spotlight pointed directly at him. Squinting, he looked to his left and his right and saw Sally on one side and Parker on the other side both tied to chairs like he was and all back in Attendant jumpsuits. Blaise was then shocked back into coherence when he realized that all three chairs were sitting on the very edge of the tower's roof, the city streets far below, but only as far as a lean just an inch too far back. His heart beat rapidly, and he began to sweat at the sight of what might as well have been an endless drop behind him.

He looked back toward the light glaring in his eyes. He could see the outlines of many Citizens standing behind the light, but no faces. Then he heard the familiar voice from the penthouse. He stepped from the shadows into the view of Blaise, Sally, and Parker, and spoke.

"It has been a tragic day for us in the towers. We have lost two of our finest and dearest at the hands of treacherous scum. Wilkins and Kurtz were the best of us in these great and mighty towers. But do not fear. I, Dr. Ambrose, will take full control. First, we will punish these insubordinate Attendants, and then...and then we will destroy the street-dwellers, and we will all exist in even greater comfort having eliminated all possible threats."

Blaise's heart sank. Not only was he going to die, but the street-dwellers would be killed anyway. Worst of all, he had gotten his...friends...killed. He paused in his thoughts. It wasn't the word "friend" that he thought of. He thought of no particular word. It was simply a vague feeling, something that he had never encountered before. He thought again of the light behind him, over the sea. And though he couldn't see it from where he was sitting, for a moment it felt warm on his back, brighter than the one beaming onto his face. For a moment he'd forgotten his imminent death.

But not for long. A Watcher in a black executioner's hood stepped into the light, walked up to Parker's chair and placed his foot on the seat. Parker squirmed in a last ditch effort to free himself, just one kick away from nothingness. Blaise looked away and closed his eyes tightly, but not so tightly that tears couldn't pour down his face.

All he could think was, *"These Towers are lower than the streets."*

CHAPTER 7

Together

When the door of the elevator shut, Nina felt a gaping hole open in her. She had felt emptiness her whole existence, but now it felt debilitating. Of all the visitors she'd ever courted into the towers, none had ever made her feel so full. And it was that newfound fullness that made the emptiness all the more potent.

She hung her head, fell back on a slot machine, and slid to the floor. Her lip quivered as she pleaded with herself not to cry. But it was no use. She sat there for a long time grieving, not wanting to stay or go; not wanting to keep crying or stop crying.

Eyes still red, she knew she had to get back to her hovel. She stood up and walked through the rows of slot machines, squinting at the bright, flashing lights, and weaving through drunken, laughing tower-dwellers. She moved more quickly as she approached the stairwell, trying hard to hold back more tears.

What was worse? Having always been empty without feeling the true depth of it, or finally feeling full only to feel emptier than she ever had? All she could think about was how it may have been better to have never met Blaise and Sally...to have never met Parker.

She opened the stairwell door, shuffled down the stairs, through the shopping area, across the bridge, made it to her floor, and finally to her cubicle. It was the longest walk of her existence. She pulled back the curtain, closed it as tightly as possible to block out any light, took off her Citizen clothes, flopped into her bed, and cried until she fell asleep.

When she woke, Dr. Ambrose's voice was over her. She shot up and looked around, but no one was there. Waking up and regaining her composure, she propped herself up on her hands, and rubbed her eyes. His voice was coming through the tower-wide speaker system.

"Citizens of these great towers; I have important and sorrowful news. Wilkins and Kurtz have been murdered. But rest assured, because the perpetrators have been quickly apprehended and will soon be executed. I alone am left to govern, and I assure you that our best days are ahead." The speaker cut to static and then off completely.

So many questions now ran through Nina's head. Could it have been Blaise, Sally, and Parker that did this? Would she too be implicated in it if they did? What should she do? That last question was the toughest one, not because she didn't know what to do, but because she knew how hard it would be to do it.

Her heart pounded, knowing that if she was going to do it, she needed help. She got up, opened the curtain, found a chair, and stood up on it. A few other Attendants who happened to be outside of their cubicles noticed her and looked at her with a puzzled glare. She took a deep breath knowing that she was about to take one of the biggest risks of her existence. As soon as the words came out, she wouldn't be able to stop, and she wouldn't be able to take the words back.

"E...every...everybody," she said. The few that watched her climb onto the chair continued looking at her with the same look. She wanted to crawl back into her hovel and never come out, but she resolved to stay where she was.

"We've only existed here in these towers. But don't you want more?" Some of those who started listening rolled their eyes and looked away. She felt discouraged, but she kept going.

"I didn't know until recently how many nice feelings there really are. I felt something I've never felt before, and it gives me the strength to stand here and tell you that it's worth fighting for."

Several other Attendants came out to see what was going on. Some of them had the slightest of hopeful looks on their faces. That gave Nina a little bit more confidence.

"We don't have to exist like this. If we work together we can be free, but it's going to be hard." Some faces frowned.

"Maybe you've never felt that there's anything worth fighting for, or maybe you have. I never realized it before now, but whenever there's a smile, whenever there's a laugh, anytime you feel like someone understands you, when they play music over the speakers and something sounds just right and your ears perk up–these are the little things that make existing worth it. And I've never wanted to fight for those things because I've been scared of losing what little I actually have. But...but I think now I'm ready to risk it because I see now that none of this is worth holding onto when I've felt a fullness I've never felt before. And chasing what makes this existence worth being a part of, even if deeper pain comes because of it, is something we should be willing to do. Come with me, and exist the way you were meant to exist!"

The room was silent. Most of the faces were blank. Many scurried back into their cubicles in fear of punishment for being associated with what she was saying. Others just slowly turned and walked. She stepped down from the chair feeling dejected. But she was determined. Whether anyone helped her or not, she was going to help Blaise, Sally, and Parker. She walked toward the stairwell door. She tried to open it, but it was jammed. As she was trying to get the door open, a finger tapped her shoulder. She was startled by ten other Attendants standing behind her. Then the one who tapped her shoulder spoke up.

"I'm 508, and we all want to help." Nina smiled and turned back to the door, suddenly finding strength to force it open. She turned back to 508 and the other Attendants.

"Come on, there's not much time."

***

Blaise sat tied to the chair; his eyes closed tightly as if to try and hold back the tears. But his eyelids were like a breaking dam. It was the end, and there was nothing he could do. He opened his eyes to look toward Sally. She was hard to see through the water in his eyes, but he could see her face, pale white and blankly staring. His heart dropped again. He couldn't bear to look back toward Parker, but nowhere his eyes led him gave him any comfort. His despair was complete. He finally looked up toward the bright spotlight pretending it was the Glow and that he had finally reached it. He closed his eyes again, and a sense of calm acceptance came over him. The moment couldn't be far away.

There was then a thud followed by a collective gasp from the onlookers. But the thud didn't come from where Parker was or from near any of the condemned, but rather from behind the crowd who had all turned to look. Some object like a rock came flying from the darkness and hit the executioner in the head. He stumbled forward and fell from the tower. Watchers readied their clubs while the crowd scattered toward the door to get off of the roof. Blaise, Sally, and Parker tried to get out of their restraints and slide their chairs away from the edge of the roof.

The three had apparently been forgotten while the Watchers focused on the assailants. But they were making no progress on untying themselves, and it could only be but so long before someone paid attention to them again.

A figure started running toward them from around the line of Watchers. It was now or never. They had to shake themselves loose, and so they all tried a little more violently to break free. Parker even succeeded in falling over on his side and clunking his head.

"Stop!" the figure yelled. To their own surprise, they obeyed it, but it was because they recognized it. Nina came into view and sighed.

"You'll hurt yourselves. Let me give you a hand."

She went first to Sally, then to Blaise, and then to Parker, untying each of them as fast as she could.

"Let's go!"

They ran to the door and saw other Attendants fighting the Watchers. At least two were already dead, and it didn't appear that the Watchers had taken any casualties. Upon getting into the door and into the stairwell, Nina gave her orders.

"Come on! Down the stairs!"

The other Attendants disengaged from the fight and retreated toward her. Blaise, Sally, Parker, Nina, and the remaining Attendants were now running for their existences downward. Their only goal was to get to the ground level and back out into the streets. They tried to barricade the door as best they could to buy some time and then they hurried down.

Fortunately, going down was much easier than going up.

"This is strange," Nina said after a while.

"Normally there would be Watchers patrolling these. I don't know where they are."

"Hardly a time to complain," said Parker.

"Maybe there's a trap on the ground floor," Sally said.

"I don't know, but let's just keep going," said Blaise.

They continued downward and downward until they finally got to the bottom. When they got there they paused before opening the door.

Nina put her ear against it. "Let's hope there's no trap on the other side."

A concerned look came across her face. "It sounds like...marching feet."

They all looked at each other puzzled.

Blaise dropped his head and shook it. "Oh no..."

He went to the door and slowly cracked it. The grand entryway, similar to the one they'd first entered through, was empty, but they could hear the sounds from outside more vividly. Orders were being yelled, and it sounded like a whole battalion of Watchers was gathering outside.

"That would explain why we didn't see any Watchers," Blaise said. "Let's go. We have to sneak around this and get back to the shore if we have any chance of surviving."

The company moved into the grand foyer, which was just as littered with trash and debris as in the tower they'd entered through. They circled through some similar office areas, expecting that they may find a way through another side window and away from the fighting taking place at the front of the building.

They entered a small room, found a window, and could see that there were no Watchers in the vicinity.

"Break it," Nina said to 508.

508 walked up with his bat, found a rag on the floor to muffle the sound, wrapped it around, and swung. The window broke easily, and 508 worked to clear some of the broken glass. They each went out the window in turn into the empty street, still hearing the sounds of marching around the corner. Once everyone was out, they ran as hard as they could. As they got around the corner of the building they saw the lines of Watchers ready to go to war. They were able to pass by unnoticed in the thickening darkness and kept up a quick pace until the Watchers were well behind them.

Where Blaise, Sally, and Parker dwelled near the shore always felt dark, but after going through what they just had, and being as close as they had been to the Deep Darkness, it felt as though the shore might as well have had daylight.

Nina, 508, and the other Attendants looked around in wonder despite still being in the bleaker part of the city not far from where Blaise, Sally, and Parker had met the camp-fire men.

"What do we do now?" Sally asked. Blaise looked up and could see the Glow in the sky ahead, but still all too distant for his liking.

"I don't know," Blaise said.

"Maybe we should go to the Arena," said Parker. "We can try and see what's going on with Mayor Max and figure out what other plans might be in motion."

Blaise found it hard to conjure the motivation he needed to care. When they'd left the Arena on their mission, he was ready to do what he needed to, but the mission had failed. They'd nearly been killed, and the war between the streets and the towers had begun anyway. It all seemed so futile now. He had no idea how to move forward except to just worry about the step in front of him and not the countless other seemingly insurmountable steps beyond that. He didn't think much would be gained from it, but he took a deep breath and sighed before speaking.

"Okay. Let's see what we can find out at the Arena."

They quickened their pace, but not by much.

CHAPTER 8

Seeing in the Dark

Blaise, Sally, Parker, Nina, 508, and the other Attendants continued to trudge through the city. Sally was lagging behind.

"Can we stop? My ankle hurts."

She leaned down and rubbed it, trying to soothe the pain.

"It hurts, but it hurts worse that I can't make it better."

Blaise stopped and looked back at her. "Okay, let's find some place to rest."

They continued a little farther down an abandoned street, scanning buildings as they went, looking through windows, and moving as cautiously as possible.

After a little while, Parker got everyone's attention. He had his face up against the window of an old row house.

"Look at this spot," he said, keeping his voice down. Nina came up behind him, put her hand on his back, and looked through the window with him.

"Looks like it'll work," she said. They looked at each other with big smiles.

Blaise walked up the crumbling steps to the door. "Let's see if we can get in."

He turned the knob and pushed. The great wooden door felt thin and light. Blaise thought he'd meet resistance, but instead the rotten wood just splintered, and before he could do anything about it, it was falling off of the hinges. The door made a loud, crashing noise onto the floor. The whole group stopped and listened for anyone or anything that may have been disturbed. No sounds came.

Sally slid past Blaise and walked into the foyer. She spun around looking up at the chandelier and into the other rooms before looking back toward the front door.

"This must've been someone's house a long time ago."

"Isn't it beautiful, Becky?" Walt said with a big grin.

She hugged him. "It's wonderful!".

The two were to be married soon, and they had just bought their first house. They stood there looking up at it for a little bit before Walt finally said, "Well, let's go inside!" He picked her up and started up the stairs. Becky giggled and hugged his neck.

The group all walked into the house. On the left through an archway was what appeared to have been a gathering area at one time. There was a couch with a broken leg and stuffing ripped out of it. A coffee table sat in front of it with a chess set on it. It looked as though a game had been interrupted. Some of the pieces had fallen over and onto the floor. But most were still standing boldly and proudly on the board, firmly in their squares, ready to continue a battle their chess-masters had long abandoned.

They all made their way into the gathering room and took seats along the walls. Blaise, Sally, and Parker shed their jumpsuits and felt better back in their regular clothes.

"How about this rundown place?" Blaise said. He looked at the couch, sitting tilted with its broken leg.

"Come sit, Walt!" Becky said with a smile. She patted the seat of their new sofa. She was wearing her favorite sundress and she was rather proud of it. Walt smiled at his lovely bride. They'd been married a year that day, and they were proud of their new purchase. But Walt didn't so much want to sit on the couch as much as he wanted to kiss her bright, warm lips. He took a puff of his pipe, snapped his suspenders, and gave her a wink. She blushed and playfully hid her face as he sat down next to her.

"I don't know. I think it's kind of nice if you can see through some of the dust," Sally said.

"This place is actually kind of a dump," said Parker. "It's worse than your little room in that overcrowded building."

Thinking of that little room gave Blaise a sense of comfort. He looked over at Sally sitting next to him. She was staring softly at the floor, but he saw the slightest grin appear on her face at its mention. He leaned a little more easily against the wall. The window on the front of the house was above his head. Looking straight up into the black sky, it didn't seem so dark for that moment. Sally's hand came to rest on Blaise's leg. He could only muster a half-grin. But he rested his hand on hers regardless, and he felt a little better. He looked over at Nina and Parker, her head on his shoulder looking as content as any two together could, even moreso than before.

Walt sat on the couch enjoying his pipe. He watched with a smile as Becky and their little daughter Claire played on the floor underneath the window. The light was shining just right. It was a pure moment. Work had been hard that day, but it seemed insignificant now. He just watched and listened to the laughing and giggling of his two favorite ladies.

He was sitting on a stain that had been on the couch now for a couple of years. Walt and Becky had been eating ravioli with red tomato sauce for dinner. Becky accidentally bumped Walt's plate and he dropped all of it onto the couch. Becky laughed as soon as it happened, but Walt wasn't so amused. He was frustrated at the damage now done, and he didn't appreciate Becky for not seeing that. Becky didn't appreciate that Walt couldn't find the humor in it. It caused a fight that night. But after a time, they just let it become a joke between them about whose fault it was that the couch was now permanently stained.

"It wouldn't be stained if you hadn't bumped my plate with your elbow!"

"Well I never would've bumped your plate if you hadn't been swinging it around so close to me!"

It was just another of the many times when joy and pain somehow existed together. It was what made life together so special for Walt and Becky. The stain was barely a thought in his mind now as he watched the two smiles he loved to see. Since the day he'd met Becky, he'd adored her smile, and seeing it had a way of melting away all of his fears, anxieties, and stresses. Their daughter's smile did the same for him. The very first time he saw it, he cried because it was her own, but also because it looked just like her mother's.

The Attendants who'd come along with 508 had been silent the whole time. Blaise, Sally, and Parker hadn't really known what to say to them, and it had been too hectic to try. Nina took her head off of Parker's shoulder, still clinging to his arm.

"Thank you," she said softly. You could tell they heard her, but none responded or even looked at her. 508 spoke up.

"These Attendants are among those who have been affected most deeply by the mistreatment. They're completely mute." He paused.

"But don't mistake their muteness for timidity. They came because they have less fear than most." They all just looked at the floor.

"Thank you," said Sally. "We would be gone without you."

"Yes. Thank you so much," Parker said. Blaise was just sitting and staring at the floor, lost in thought. After a long pause, Sally nudged him slightly to get him to speak up.

Walt shuffled into the family room. Becky was resting on their beloved old couch. Walt's cane clicked on the floor as he stepped into the room. Becky's face was wrinkled, and her hair was white, but her smile was as beautiful to him as it ever was. Her health had been failing over the past several months, but she was grateful for the life she'd lived. Claire was arriving for dinner shortly with her husband and children. She'd been busy lately, so they hadn't seen her in a while. She lived across the water and didn't make it over as often as any of them liked. Walt eased himself slowly onto the couch next to her, leaning on his cane as he lowered himself. Walt gave her a little unsealed envelope with a folded up piece of paper inside. She took it out and read it eagerly. When she put it down, she saw Walt trying to speak.

"Thank you," Walt said through tears.

"Thank you," Becky said with her same lovely smile.
"Thank you," Blaise finally uttered.

***

Blaise woke up still leaning against the wall in the old house. Sally's head was resting on his lap, still sleeping. He lifted his hand and moved it over her head, but hesitated before letting his hand fall gently on her soft, smooth hair. She stirred as he ran his fingers through it. He pulled his hand away, but she didn't wake up. Everyone was still sleeping, and Blaise didn't feel much like waking everyone up, or doing anything at all, but he decided it was time.

"We'd better go," Blaise said, breaking the silence in the room. One by one everyone began waking up, rubbing their eyes, yawning, and groaning. Sally sat up and let out a sigh. There was heaviness in the air, but they knew that they had to keep going. Blaise let everyone go ahead of him as they all shuffled out of the building. He looked at the old, tattered couch one more time, not sure what to think of it, but glad to have had a place to rest. Blaise stepped outside. Everyone else was standing on the sidewalk.

"Let's get to the Arena."

They moved through the city, and as they got closer to the shore, it remained eerily silent.

"Something's off," Sally said with a furled brow.

"It seems like there are fewer street-dwellers around than normal."

"We better watch our backs," Parker chimed in.

They started looking around corners before going around

them but they didn't see anyone at all. A couple of blocks from the Arena they heard some noises come from its direction.

"What's going on?" Sally said.

"It sounds like...weeping and wailing," said Nina.

They moved even more cautiously as they approached. Blaise walked up to the last corner and looked around it. There was a large group of street-dwellers crying together, but Blaise couldn't quite see what else was going on. He peeked around some more and saw bloody bodies lying in the street. He moved out from cover and walked over with the others following. The mourners didn't pay much attention to them as they walked toward them. One of the mourners was muttering something about "the horrid tower-dwellers." But it appeared that the mourners only found them dead and didn't see what happened. Blaise stepped toward one of the dead in the street to examine them.

There were deep slashes in all of the bodies. Many had puncture wounds that went straight through their chests to their backs.

"A sword..."

He made a nervous gulp and looked at the door to the Arena. He looked back at the rest of the group, nodded, and they followed him toward it. They had to step over and through the bodies to get to it. The journey toward the door was short but grueling, and the thought of seeing what was behind it was no consolation. Blaise slowly opened it. It was worse than he could have imagined. The dead were lying everywhere. On the concourse, in the seats, and down on the floor. He could see straight through to the ring in the middle.

Many of Mayor Max's henchmen lay dead in the center. Blaise turned and vomited.

The mourners were now getting rowdy and began loudly calling for the end of the towers. Cheers and chants broke out, and Blaise started to feel dizzy. He threw up again. Holding his stomach, he walked away from the door and started pushing through the growing crowd. Stumbling, he made it out into the open air, but still felt as though he couldn't breathe. He looked back toward the crowd who was still chanting for war. The others made their way out of the crowd trying to get to Blaise. He saw the concerned look on Sally's face as he lost balance and fell over. Sally got to him and crouched down next to him.

"Are you okay!?"

She was trying to rub his back and hug him, but Blaise moved away from them all, scooting on his butt as fast as it would take him while trying to get a breath. He stumbled to his feet and his mind went to one thing. He ran as fast as he could to the overlook.

But, on his way, he had a dark thought and decided to stop somewhere else first. Blaise now ran to his and Sally's building. Bailey had a look of shock on his face as Blaise threw open the door and ran up the stairs. Without a second thought, he trampled the game the kids were playing. He opened the door to his room as the children wailed "What was that for?" and "What a jerk!"

The door slammed into the bed, and looking toward the window, he saw it: The Bright pill still sitting on the sill. He pushed out all of his thoughts telling him not to take it. Indignant, he went to it and picked it up. After barely even a moment of hesitation, he put it in his mouth and swallowed it.

Everything around him was shimmering, though he also felt lower and darker. Sweat pooled on his brow, and he was breathing heavily. The tension flowed out of him, but it felt cheap. He stumbled out of the room, down the stairs, and continued toward the overlook.

Once Blaise got there, he looked in the direction of the Glow, angrier at it now than he'd ever been, but also wanting the Glow more than he ever had. The Bright made it harder to distinguish since everything now looked like artificial light. Looking in its direction now, it felt like a falsehood. A figment of his imagination. It didn't exist, yet he was angry at it for not existing.

He jumped over the wall and down onto the beach. He found the old row boat tucked down next to the wall where he'd left it and dragged it to the water. He got in and started rowing as hard as he could. As he started, he saw Sally and the others arrive at the overlook. Sally's hand went over her mouth, and he felt guilty at having worried her another time, but this time he was determined to row and row as hard as he could whatever the result.

He got to the same fifty yard point he'd gotten to twice before and he rowed even harder. Water was spilling into the boat and dripping down his face. He was soaked to the bone, but he was in a battle, and he wouldn't be deterred. The same large wave appeared, but he stayed committed to his goal. The wave didn't swallow him. Then, much to his surprise, he made it to the top of the crest. He kept rowing, and even more to his surprise, he got over the wave. He felt a moment of pride and victory. He let out a victorious yell. But while he relished the victory a wall of water struck him from behind, and everything went dark.

Blaise heard sobbing as he started to regain consciousness. Everything was dark, and he felt awful. His head hurt first, and then he started to feel pain all over his body. He could tell that he was lying on his back in a bed, and felt something resting on his chest. As he stirred awake, the crying stopped, and what was resting on his chest moved away. His eyes were still closed, but he now knew it was someone's head. He slowly opened his eyes and saw Sally's face looking back at him. Tears were still on her face, but there was eagerness in her eyes. Her tears of sadness turned to tears of joy and she drew closer to hug him around the neck.

"I thought I'd lost you."

Blaise could now tell that they were in their room when a knock came at the door.

"Come in," Sally said. It opened and Bailey's face peeked around.

"I see our boy's come around," he said.

Sally smiled at Blaise. "Bailey helped get you back here, and patch you up."

"Glad to see you're awake, and glad to see some happy tears for once. I'll be back soon to check on ya," Bailey said as he closed the door.

Blaise looked back at Sally. She was facing the door, sitting on the edge of the bed next to him with a soft smile and a few tears still on her cheek. And then for the first time, Blaise didn't just look at Sally, he let her in. As if for the first time, he saw her soft cheeks, her long, flowing hair, and the smile that had gotten him through so much. Seeing her smile had always kept him going when things felt dark. But now for the first time, bruised and beaten, he reconciled with his wounds, and gave in to his feelings.

Without fear, he picked up his hand and placed it on her cheek. She turned and smiled, and looked relieved. Then he uttered the only words he knew to say.

"You're so much."

Sally blushed. "So are you."

Blaise tried to sit up further in the bed. He pushed himself up with great pain.

"What are you doing? You're hurt." He leaned forward and pulled her closer. She smiled again, knowing what he wanted. He kissed her, and this time he felt it. He knew he'd always liked kissing her lips, but now it really meant something. They were a part of one another.

They sat and talked on deeper levels than they ever had. They laughed and cried for a long time. They hugged and kissed, and sometimes just sat in silence. Blaise could see the Glow outside. He couldn't decide whether it really was closer or if it just felt that way, but it didn't really matter.

***

Sally was resting her head on Blaise's chest when there was a knock at the door. Bailey opened it and shuffled in.

"Morning," he said with a glum look on his face.

"You can hear the sounds of fighting off in the distance more clearly now."

Blaise furled his brow and looked down.

"What's been happening?"

Sally sighed.

"There's a lot to tell. After the wave hit you, you were lying on the beach badly hurt. So we were able to get you here, and then Bailey helped get you on the mend."

She paused, and tears formed in her eyes. "But we weren't sure if you'd ever wake up."

After wiping her eyes and gathering herself, she continued. "While you were out, things got worse. Street-dwellers were yelling about going to war while others hid in fear. It's been tense. Not only that, more and more street-dwellers are dying from Bright."

Blaise tried to process it all. "Where are...where are Parker and Nina?"

"They were here, but they left to fight. The main battle is farther in toward the Towers. Not many have come back from there, so we're not sure exactly what's happening...except that the sounds of battle are getting louder and closer."

Blaise let out a sigh and would have cried if he had any energy left to do so. Waking up in the dark city always seemed to mean waking up to bad news, but it seemed to him as though the end really was near this time. He reached for Sally's hand and gripped it tightly.

Bailey shifted as he stood listening. "Uh...Sally told me that you'd seen a dark figure with a sword."

"Yes."

Bailey stammered. "I...I'm not sure, but I think I might know something about it."

Both Blaise and Sally looked up at him, intrigued.

"Why didn't you say anything when I first mentioned it?"

"Well I wasn't too sure, and I didn't want to say too much. It was a long time ago, and I don't remember the book or even a lot of the details. But I once read a legend about the so-called 'Prince of the Deep Darkness.'"

The air in the room felt heavier, and Blaise and Sally felt entranced by what he was saying.

"They say he's the quiet ruler of the dark city, the one who keeps it that way by his terrible forces. He doesn't rule in the open for all to see. He rules by bending us to his will, by working in the shadows, only coming out of his lair in the Deep Darkness to do his horrible deeds. Most haven't even heard of him, and if they have they don't believe he's real...and that's the way he likes it."

A cold breeze went through the room.

"He caused this whole war," Blaise said in a whisper. "If that black figure was the Prince of the Deep Darkness like you said, then he killed Wilkins and started this whole thing. Then he came and massacred everyone at the Arena. Everyone just assumed it was the tower-dwellers."

There was a long silence before Blaise remembered something. He started searching through his pockets, desperately hoping it was still there. He pulled out the piece of paper that he had folded up and taken from the file in the Towers and held it out to Bailey.

"Can you read this?"

"What...what is it?" He took it from Blaise and began unfolding it.

"It got a little wet, but I'll see what I can do."

Blaise's chest was pounding with excitement, and Sally glanced between them trying to figure out what was going on.

"Let's see here. It says 'Summary.' Then after that it says..."

The Glow phenomenon has been the object of a tremendous amount of thought and belief. Numerous tests have been performed to unlock its secrets, yet it eludes all experimentation. It cannot be reached by physical means, and does not appear to affect us in any natural way. The illusion that it does shed light on us is mistaken. Any light we possess here can be accounted for by means other than the Glow. Because it cannot be reached or studied, it is therefore merely a non-existent entity. It is a figment of the imagination or, at best, the Glow is a reflection of the light that emanates from the shore. Interest in it should be reserved for those of weak mind or those interested in influencing weak minds. The Glow project is hereby closed, an initiative for which I took exception from the start, but humored for the sake of less sophisticated minds.

Signed, Dr. H.A. Eldridge

There was a long silence. Bailey quietly folded the paper, put it down on the bed, and tried not to make eye contact. Sally looked right at Blaise, her eyes wide and jaw hanging open. She gripped his hand tightly and waited for his response.

He hung his head and shook it. "I...I don't believe that. I can't believe that. I...I don't know...maybe...but...I can't. I won't."

Looking up at Sally, he realized what he needed to do: go into the Deep Darkness to confront the Prince. He knew he may never reach the Glow, that, at best, the darkness would consume him and make him into a Deep One, and that, at worst, he would die, but he would at least die trying to preserve the city.

Just as he made his decision to go, he remembered something else: his failure at the towers. He'd set out to stop the war and failed. The weight of that thought made him want to stop before starting. But finding what he did with Sally put more fight in him. So making his mind up a second time, he resolved to go. That's how it is, anyway. Making up one's mind to do something doesn't really mean making it up once; it means making it up over and over again. And so he resolved to do that too.

"Do you know how to get to the Prince?" Blaise asked.

"No," Bailey answered.

"Would anyone know?" Blaise asked.

"None that you could easily talk to," said Bailey.

"But legend says that the 'Deep Ones' serve him. If you find one of them, you'll find him."

Blaise looked at Sally, and Sally looked back at him.

"I have to do this."

"Okay....I know we can."

"But not 'we.' I can't put you in any more danger."

Her brow furled and a fire lit in her eyes.

"I'm going with you. I'm never leaving your side."

Blaise felt warm, and he smiled. There was no point in arguing with her.

But there was still another problem. Blaise hadn't gotten out of bed in some time. He felt much better than he did when he first woke up, but he hadn't tried to stand up or walk. He slowly started to move his feet toward the edge of the bed. He was sore, but he felt like he could do it. He got his feet on the floor and tried to stand up, but he lost strength and sat back down. Sally then moved in front of him and hugged him under his arms to help pull him up. He felt another wind of strength come over him.

"Come on. You can do it," she said.

"One...Two...THREE." On three he tried to stand. Sally pulled him up, and he managed to get to his feet. They smiled at each other, and Blaise rested his forehead on hers.

"Thanks."

Blaise stretched and tried to take a few steps. It took a little bit of moving around to loosen up, but he felt better pretty quickly. Blaise looked at Sally.

"Let's go find the Prince."

They shuffled sideways out of the room and down the stairs. They moved fairly slowly. Blaise was still sore, and so was Sally's ankle. They were hurting, but they were together.

When they opened the door to the outside there was turmoil all around. There were more dead street-dwellers lying around than ever before. Many others were obviously on Bright. The hurt in the city was growing. Strangely enough though, Blaise looked up at the Glow. It was...flickering.

Blaise and Sally hurried down the stairs, ran down the sidewalk, and around the corner. In front of them were the towers off in the distance where they'd been not long before. Something was different about them though. The Deep Darkness had moved. The Towers looked like they were being swallowed by it. Blaise looked back at the Glow. He still saw the flickering in it, but he also noticed something else. It too had grown closer to the shore.

CHAPTER 9

Not by Sight

Blaise and Sally were moving as quickly and stealthily as they could. They were going the long way around so that they could avoid the battle. They were checking around each building before passing it, sometimes seeing small battles, but most often they'd just see altercations well off in the distance. The towers were growing taller as they approached them. Though now the Deep Darkness appeared to almost entirely mask them.

They started moving more slowly the closer they approached, knowing what they needed to do, but not really wanting to reach their destination.

"We're almost there," Blaise said with no enthusiasm.

Sally clung to his arm. "Just one step at a time."

It wasn't long enough before they were staring up at the Deep Darkness. When they first saw it they had hoped never to see it so close again. Now their task required more than they could handle.

Blaise and Sally were now no more than ten yards from that deathly wall. Their fear multiplied with each slowing step. But they were determined. They took one step, mustered their courage for another, took a half step back, breathed deeply, and took another small step forward. To them, it seemed that no one had ever taken so much time to travel such a small distance.

Eventually they stood with their noses to the blackness, holding each other's hands as tightly as they could. They slowly turned toward one another, eyes wide, and filled with fear. Blaise saw Sally trembling. Despite what she had said, he felt another twinge of guilt for putting her in danger. But of course, she smiled at him, softly and simply. Blaise felt the strength come back into him.

"Ready?"

"Just waiting on you," Sally said with a sly smile. They took a deep breath and plunged into the Deep Darkness.

Blaise and Sally took more steps forward. They couldn't see a single thing in front of them, but they knew they must keep walking. It had to be slow-going or else they might have run into something. Even at their feet, they knew they were stepping on the road, but they couldn't even see their shoes or where their feet were landing. It was as if they were somehow standing in a void with no ground under them, but there was after all.

After walking about a block, they looked backward. They could see where the Deep Darkness ended, and even though it was dark in the city, the difference between it and the Deep Darkness looked similar to that between the dark city and the Glow.

"I wonder if the Deep Ones think the city is actually bright," Blaise said.

Blaise and Sally turned and kept walking. They couldn't even see each other, but they could hear each other. When they weren't talking the only way they each knew the other was there was by the tight grip they had on each other's hands. It didn't change what they were dealing with, but it made it more bearable, and so they trudged forward at all costs. One step at a time.

"It's kind of like wading into the cold sea," Blaise said. "At first you're scared, but you get in anyway. Even then, it's uncomfortable, but it gets easier."

Sally squeezed his hand.

To continue moving was the only option. It didn't cross their minds so much that they didn't know where they were going. Somehow they knew they'd find their way. There was a long, focused silence before either of them spoke again.

Then Blaise, almost in a whisper, said, "And we complain about how dark it is near the shore. It would be great to have that much light to see by now."

"Hmm," said Sally. "I guess the more light we have, the less we appreciate it. In this kind of darkness we have no other option other than to...trust."

But regardless, the further they moved without any light, the more daunting it became.

"Why did we do this? What were we thinking?"

These were the thoughts that came across their minds. They kept trudging through what they thought must have been two or three blocks.

"What's that up ahead?" Sally said.

"I'm not sure."

"They look like columns of light."

"I didn't think we'd find any light here at all, but I think you're right," Blaise said.

"I'm not sure what they're coming from though."

Whatever it was, it looked like the columns of light were all in a row shining up the street for some distance at set intervals.

"Let's get a closer look," Sally suggested.

They started to move a little more quickly toward the first column, forgetting for a moment that they could trip on any number of things in the road. As they approached, they started to slow down. Blaise stepped toward one.

"They're manholes!"

He then covered his mouth realizing that this could be a lair of the Deep Ones. They paused in silence for a moment and heard nothing coming from below. Blaise then stepped carefully toward it to get a look inside. He peeked down and saw what looked like a tunnel down below.

"I'm going to get a closer look," Blaise said as he put his foot on the rung of the ladder.

"Be careful."

Blaise took a few steps down and didn't see anyone. Hanging from the ladder, he saw torches on the walls of a long tunnel about the size of a subway tunnel. The tunnel curved such that he couldn't see all that far down it, but it appeared to be a passage frequently used by someone. Blaise climbed back up the ladder.

"What do you think?" Sally asked.

"I think it's our best bet," Blaise responded. "But who knows what we may face down there?"

"I think it's our *only* bet," Sally said.

"Let's go then."

Blaise climbed back down the ladder and Sally followed. They got all the way to the bottom and peered down the tunnel. They had enough dim light to see each other now, but they held each other's hands all the same.

They went down the tunnel feeling more fearful than even before. In the darkness they weren't sure they'd ever find their destination, and perhaps they had taken some comfort in that. As their chances of finding the Prince grew, so did their fear.

Their feet sloshed through water and muck, soaking their shoes. It smelled musty and damp most of the way, but they liked that better than the foul smelling stench that ocassionally wafted into their nostrils as they walked.

As they went, they surprisingly found themselves laughing and smiling again. The fear was still there, but that's no excuse to be miserable. Then Blaise felt something well up in him that he'd never felt before. It was new and powerful, but he still didn't quite understand it. He just knew he should speak.

"Sally, I..."

She blushed in the torchlight. "You hardly ever call me by my name."

"Oh. I'm...I'm sorry."

"No, it's okay. I liked it."

Sally watched Blaise look down and scratch his head.

"Why do you seem so nervous? What's wrong?"

"I don't know. I'm okay. I'm feeling something, and I don't know what it is."

"Is it a bad feeling?"

"No. It's not bad. It's...important.... And so I'm nervous, but even if I wasn't, I can't find the words."

They stopped walking and turned toward each other.

"I think I...I think I feel it too. I've felt it for a long time, but right now it's even stronger. It's like there are words I want to say, but can't."

"Exactly...."

They stood there just staring at each other, itching to get the words out. Blaise watched Sally's lips quiver as she fought to speak.

"I..." Then she turned.

"What's that?"

Coming from behind them in the tunnel were the sounds of an army of feet splashing through water. They heard snarling, howling, and other terrifying noises.

Sally looked back at Blaise. "...Deep Ones."

"Run!"

Hand in hand, they ran as fast as they could, but the noises were still getting closer. Blaise spotted a nook to hide in.

"There!" he said. But as they changed course, Sally let out a scream and fell to the ground.

"I think I hurt my ankle again."

"We have to hide!"

Sally tried to stand but her ankle gave out. Blaise leaned down to pick her up, but as he did, a hoard of Deep Ones came around the bend. They were dirty, disheveled. Some were even crawling on all fours. They looked like mindless shells. Their eyes were filled with darkness.

The stampede was upon them. Blaise and Sally were jostled away from each other. He tried to maintain a grip on her but they were ripped apart. Blaise felt himself tumble around and get stepped on several times before coming to a halt face down on a mound of mud. He was disoriented, but he was able to lift his head just enough to see Sally draped over the shoulder of a Deep One and carried off down the tunnel.

***

Parker couldn't remember how many sleep cycles it had been since he and Nina arrived at the barricaded intersection that served as a base for the street-dwellers. He sat leaning up against an old desk aching and exhausted. Nina looked over at him with concerned glances as she tended to the wounded nearby. Others were scowling at him as they walked. All Parker could do was stare at the asphalt and wonder whether the drops of liquid sliding down his face were sweat or blood.

He had barely made it back over the main barricade as a large band of Watchers charged it. Many of those standing near him had been swiftly beaten down and killed, but Parker had managed to scramble backward enough to miss the worst of it. As Parker ran back he heard another street-dweller yell, "Where are you go...?" before the same man screamed and fell.

The street-dwellers had managed to defend the barricade so far, but it wouldn't be long before the Watchers would break through and overrun them. There had been murmurings about reinforcements, but none had come. All watched nervously as more street-dwellers were climbing back into the camp than were heading out into battle. 508 and some of the other Attendants were among the few on their way into the battle. As 508 disappeared over the barricade, a battle-worn street-dweller, bloodied and bruised appeared coming back over it.

"The Watchers," he said, trying to catch his breath. "They're...they're just on the other side!"

Parker looked at the ground and then back at Nina. She was already looking back at him. He felt the darkness creeping in, and yet Nina's eyes gave him strength. All his existence he had been what he was, but he had never been ashamed of it...until Nina. He could bear it no longer. He sat up a little taller and knew there was only one thing to do. He got up and walked over to her.

He put his hands on her shoulders.

"Nina. Gather the wounded and enough street-dwellers to carry them and make for the shore." Her eyes got wide.

"I'll stay here and meet them when they come through and help give you enough time to escape."

"No!" she cried as she moved to hug him tightly. "Help me with the wounded."

"No. I have to do this," Parker said. "I've always run away when things got tough. It's time to stand up. If I leave, I'll still die.. But I'll die a coward. If I stay..."

There was a long pause as they heard the barricade start to rattle.

"You're my best," Nina said. It was all she knew to say.

"So are you. Now, Go...Go!"

Nina, through tears, mustered her strength. She gulped

and pulled away. When their hands broke contact, it was like the wind was knocked out of their lungs. Neither could breathe, but both had a purpose.

"Gather all the injured! We need to leave. You! Carry him. You two! Help him!" Nina started leading all of the injured toward the back barricade. It was slow going getting everyone over it, but they were making steady progress.

Parker walked into the crowd of fighters standing near the rattling barricade. "What do we do?" one of them asked another. But none of the street-dwellers spoke. Parker gathered the courage to say what he was thinking.

"This city isn't much, but it's ours. When that barricade breaks, I say we fight to the last man. Because we are more than just the trash they see us as and that we've believed ourselves to be. Let's prove it to them!"

They looked at him skeptically at first, but then came the silent nods of approval. The barricade rattled again, and some items fell off of the top. 508 scrambled over. Parker looked back. Nina was standing on top of the back barricade. All of the injured had made it. They looked at each other. Nina smiled, and Parker smiled back.

The main barricade broke. Parker looked toward it, and Watchers started pouring through. He looked back toward Nina, and she was gone. His full heart sank, but the fullness was now more powerful than the sinking.

"Charge!" he cried. The street dwellers and 508 ran at the Watchers. Parker managed to wrestle a bat out of the hands of one of them and make some strikes with it. He watched as street-dwellers were beaten down and killed, but they kept up the pressure. Parker was swinging at any Watcher who got near him. He felt right.

But the Watchers quickly took control. Parker and the street-dwellers were driven into the center of the camp and surrounded. He stood shoulder to shoulder with 508. Both were standing tall and proud. Things went silent and moved in slow-motion as a Watcher raised his bat. Parker took in his surroundings: the dark sky, the trash, the rubble, and decay. None of it bothered him. He had fought for what little it was, and that's what mattered. The last thing he saw was a few heavily sooted men with scraggly beards appear over one of the barricades. A smile came across his face.

"Reinforcements," he whispered.

But all too late he knew. As the stroke fell Parker felt a peace he'd never felt before. He'd caught glimpses of it in Nina's eyes, but never like this. Her smiling face flashed before him. The light was pure and overwhelming.

***

When Blaise woke up the Deep Ones were gone, and everything was quiet. He had a moment of peace at that thought before he remembered that they had taken Sally. He got up as quickly as he could, still sore from both tumbling to shore in the boat and now the stampede.

As he stood, pain filled his lower leg. He had only a vague recollection of a Deep One stepping on it. Blaise hobbled over to the wall and fell into it, slamming his cheek on the hard rock. He touched it and looked at the blood now on his finger. But he had no time to tend to his wounds. Using the wall as a crutch, he started walking down the tunnel.

Guided only by the torches, he dragged his feet and sobbed, determined to get wherever Sally was and thinking of her as the destination rather than the Prince.

Blaise went around twists and turns, always careful to look around the corner to see if there was anything there. The loneliness and fear was setting in so deeply that he wished against all hope that Sally was there waiting around each turn. But when she wasn't, he'd almost wish to see another Deep One just so he didn't have to be by himself. Maybe he'd even be lucky enough for the Deep One to end his misery. Each time he had those thoughts, he tried to push them out and think of the things that made him feel better. The Glow, of course, was one of them, but it only appeared in the background of his thoughts about the simple days on the overlook, Parker, Bailey, even Nina, but mostly Sally.

As he went along, not sure he'd ever find his way out, he came to a steep decline in the tunnel. A steady stream of water was flowing out of the wall nearby and draining down into it. There were no torches at the bottom, but he could see a little bit of light from the other side that revealed part of an incline back up. Blaise took a deep breath and carefully placed his uninjured foot on the ramp trying to get a grip. Despite the water that was getting into his shoes, he was encouraged by a few well-placed steps. But they didn't last. He had one bad step on a slippery rock and he slid all the way to the bottom, landing in mud. All he could do was lay there for a few moments and gather himself.

"I can do this. It'll be okay."

Sitting back, he could see all the way to the top of the incline in front of him and the torches that showed him the way.

"That doesn't seem so bad."

He used the wall to stand up again and tried to slog through the mud. At the base of the incline, he got his footing and began trying to climb. There wasn't much to hold on to, but he just tried to focus on finding whatever grip he could with his hands and use his uninjured foot to hop up. He was scared his foot would slip and he would slide back into the mud, but the closer he got to the top, the better he felt.

"Almost there. Almost there."

But just as he was about to reach the top, his foot slipped, and he slid right back down into the mud. He just laid there with his feet stuck in the muck, his forehead on the ramp, and began to sob.

"Why? Why? Why? Why? WHY?"

It may have been one slip, but the entire weight of Blaise's existence landed on him at that moment, and all kinds of thoughts filled his mind.

"Why does nothing just work? Not the boat. Not my plans. Everything is mud and garbage. I might as well stay here. There's no point in going on. I'll never get to the Glow. I'll never see Sally again. This is where it ends."

Blaise went through a long cycle of frustration, anger, despair, and then a moment of calm. With his nose still pressed against the ground, the musty dirt of the tunnel started to get his attention. It wasn't a pleasant smell, but it distracted him from his thoughts just long enough to remind him that he was still breathing. And as he laid there it started to smell familiar, but he couldn't quite place why.

"I must be delirious. What is this smell?"

When he remembered, it all rushed in at once. It was the way his and Sally's room smelled when they first walked into it. It wasn't, of course, a memory that would mean a thing to anyone else. But then again, many of one's most precious memories are this way. He remembered them both smiling despite having to wave away the smell with their hands. They laughed about it for a while, and it was even longer before they no longer noticed it. He looked up at the torches still flickering at the top of the incline.

"Home is where we both are," is what she said that day. Those words almost felt audible again. Blaise rubbed away some dirt and got back up. He crawled up again, this time using his hurt leg too. Battling through the pain, he just focused on getting to the top. About halfway up he slipped again, but only a little. His hurt leg stopped his skid, and he screamed in pain.

"I must keep going."

Up and up, little by little. The spot where he had fallen before was just in front of him. He tried holding on to some different spots this time and made more progress than he had before. Just a little bit more is all he needed. His first hand reached the landing, and then the second. He started to move his foot up to the landing, but his bad foot slipped again, and he began to slide back down.

"No. No. NO!"

With all the strength he still had left, he clamored to keep his hands on the landing. One hand slipped off, and he gripped as hard as he could with the other, but he was losing strength in his fingers. There was nothing he could do to stop from slipping. His fingers were about to give out, but he refused to give up. In a risky maneuver he swung his other hand back up and was able to get a grip. He pulled himself up using only his arms this time. It was more difficult, but with another big heave, he was laying on the top of the landing.

'Yes!... Yes Yes YES!" He had not just conquered the incline, but felt as though he crossed the sea. His despair melted away as he tasted victory for what felt like the first time.

But elation soon gave way to a calm focus. Blaise picked himself off the floor and peered down a much more narrow tunnel with far more space between torches.

"One step at a time."

He put one foot ahead of the other. And almost to his surprise, his feet didn't stop. He was more determined than he was afraid.

"Sally...Sally...Sally...."

There were other inclines and declines, other twists and turns, areas that were dark and damp, and those that were light and dry. Then came a long, dark, straight passage that appeared to open into a lighted room far at the other end. Blaise put his head down and ran as fast as he could, keeping his eyes on the room ahead. Mud slowed him down at a few points, but he just kept slogging through it as determined as ever. As the room grew nearer he ran even faster, both to reach the light of the room and to escape the darkness of the tunnel. Just before reaching it, he tripped on something at the very end of the passage and stumbled into the room before hitting the ground hard.

"No time to waste," he thought as he pushed himself back up to a sitting position. His face and hands were hurt from the fall, but he dusted himself off and looked around. Torches lined the walls. Moreso than in any other place in the tunnel, and bigger ones too. But most prominent was the ladder in the middle of the room that appeared to lead up to another manhole. He got to his feet and stepped toward it and looked up. Not really wanting to know what he would find at the top, he grabbed hold of the rung in front of him and started to climb.

Just before his head came out of the manhole, he peeked carefully to see if anyone was around. The menacing sight caught him off guard. Before him was the unmistakable outline of a dark and ominous cathedral. Giant torches hung on the spires and near the entryway, giving light enough to see it. He'd never seen a building like it. It was an ornate cathedral with intricate architecture and a towering presence.

Blaise couldn't hear anyone else around, so he slowly lifted himself out of the manhole and started approaching it as cautiously as he could. He started up the grand staircase to the mighty building's entrance. To his surprise, he could see that the door was wide open, though it was completely black inside.

"Sally must be in there. I have to find her."

He mustered his courage and put his shoulder down to enter the blackness of the cathedral as if he were trying to break it open.

The darkness in the cathedral somehow felt even thicker than walking into the Deep Darkness for the first time. Blaise couldn't believe that there was anything worse. But he kept moving. He felt some sense of comfort in having the torch light outside. But just as he had that thought, the doors slammed shut. He gasped and froze. Then torches started igniting at different points along the walls of the cathedral. The great, dark sanctuary was revealed.

There were great columns that led all the way up to the high ceiling. Tattered artwork lined the walls. Pews filled with Deep Ones led all the way up to the altar. On that altar was a throne, and on that throne was the Prince. Blaise recognized that dark figure immediately as the one he'd seen in the towers. The Prince remained silent on the throne, but his mask was directed at Blaise.

Blaise marched cautiously up the aisle, trying to build his confidence as he went. The Deep Ones snarled and screamed at him, or simply glared at him with their empty eyes, but stayed where they were.

The shadowy figure remained still, his face still hidden behind a mask, and his body still in a dark cloak. Blaise couldn't see the sword, but he knew it must be close. He got to within a few paces from the throne, and he could now see that whatever the Prince was, he was unnaturally large. Much larger than any normal man.

To his surprise, Blaise made it all the way up the aisle unhindered. The Prince only reacted by turning his cloaked head a little to the right and staring in that direction. Blaise was hesitant to take his eyes off of the Prince, but slowly turned his own head to look. There, lying on the first pew, was Sally, her hands and feet tied and with a gag in her mouth.

He wanted to run to her, but before he could take a step he was stopped cold in his tracks by the voice of the Prince.

To his surprise, the voice didn't strike fear in him. It was actually...comforting, but not in the right way. Blaise could feel a tension in it and himself. What was also disconcerting was that it felt as though the voice was coming from inside his own mind.

"I thought you'd arrive soon."

Blaise turned to look at him. "You..you did?"

"It is a great pleasure to be pursued, is it not? And you have been seeking me for quite some time."

"I wanted to find you...so that the war would stop, and so that you would stop spreading all your horrors."

"No. No. That's not it. You've been searching for me for much longer than that."

"But I..."

"Rather, you've been searching for what you know I can give you..."

Blaise could only whisper it. "The Glow."

"Of course," he thought. Who else in the city could have that power? His mouth was watering at the thought of getting to where he'd always wanted to be, and an unnatural warmth came over him.

"Can you really take me to the Glow?"

"I can."

"How?"

"Because I came from the Glow."

Blaise was now enthralled.

"What do I have to do to get there?"

"You must make a choice."

Blaise gulped.

"Both of you must bow to me and swear to serve me, and I

will take you to the Glow. There you won't starve, you won't struggle, and you won't be threatened. Your dirt and grime will be gone."

Blaise felt his knees buckle. But the Prince paused and Blaise felt a cold wind.

"But if you do not bow to me, I will kill you both and swallow the city in Deep Darkness. The choice could not be more clear."

And Blaise felt that way too. Death or everything he'd ever wanted? No question was in his mind.

Before Blaise could do anything, The Prince raised his arm just slightly, and the cathedral shook. Blaise turned to look at Sally. Her restraints disintegrated and the Prince lowered his arm.

Blaise ran to her as she sat up. Her eyes looked teary as he sat next to her, but he was beaming with delight.

"Did you hear that, Sally?"

She wiped her eyes and softly said, "Yes, I heard it."

"What's wrong?"

"Blaise. I...I won't do it. I won't bow to him."

Blaise shot up. "What are you talking about? The Glow or death? Why wouldn't we choose the Glow?"

He just looked down at her and into her flooded eyes, tears starting to spill over onto her cheek.

"Th...Think about it, Blaise," she said in a whisper. "Look at all that he's done. He kills and captures, hides in the shadows and darkness, manipulates and enslaves, and promises empty pleasures."

Blaise's heart softened, and the tension ran out of him.

And through her tears she said, "No one who brings such darkness can have anything to do with the light."

Blaise dropped his head. Of course, she was right. They nodded at each other knowing what they must do. Blaise took Sally's hand as she stood, and they both turned to face the prince, hand in hand. They filled their chests as if in a last act of defiance before the headsman's ax fell.

"No," Blaise said.

To the Prince, it sounded no louder than a whisper, but to Blaise and Sally it was almost deafening.

When the "No" rang out, Blaise had a flash of images go through his mind. He remembered all the times that he had seen Sally's smile, he saw the care of Bailey, the looks between Nina and Parker, and the Glow in the background behind it all.

The Prince stood up and drew his sword from under his cloak. He was no longer calming or comforting as he towered above them. The shadowy figure raised his sword over his head. Blaise gripped Sally's hand, both knowing that they were powerless to defend themselves. They bowed their heads, closed their eyes, and waited for the end to come.

But it didn't. After more moments than they thought should have been left, they were...alive. A still silence had fallen over the cathedral. Blaise opened his eyes, and kept his head down, but he looked at Sally who was looking back at him. Slowly looking up, they saw that the Prince had stepped back, sword at his side, and masked face looking toward the door.

The cathedral began to shake, but rather than collapse, it began to reconstruct itself. Fallen columns moved back into place, the ceiling's painting became more clear, and in the doorway stood another figure masked in shadow, not because he was shadow, but because the Glow shone behind him.

CHAPTER 10

The Light

Nina was moving as quickly as possible back to the shore. Parker had bought them time to escape, but they weren't safe yet if they were ever going to be at all. Nina was trying to put out of her mind what was likely Parker's fate. All she could do was focus on the task at hand. One slow-going step after slow-going step with almost all of the weight of an injured street-dweller she was supporting as they walked. Nina turned her head to look at his face. Dry blood covered it. He was hunched over and clutching his side. His other arm was over Nina's shoulder. She began to say something but decided not to. There was no consolation. The man just looked down at the ground with a wide-eyed and unbroken stare. Nina turned her head forward again and just continued thinking about her steps.

The group eventually met up with another set of retreating street soldiers who were also going back toward the shore. Nina let out a sigh of relief at their sight. They came over and started helping carry the load of the injured. Someone came up to Nina and took over carrying the man she was helping. The reprieve from the physical weight momentarily relieved her of the emotional weight. She rolled and stretched her neck and back before continuing on with the now expanded party. It was nice to see other faces, but it was discouraging too. This other group was a last remnant. The battle was nearly over. Their doom was waiting. They all silently understood this.

"Let's go look at the Glow," Nina suggested. The mood was somber, but they continued forward. They soon came to that great overlook. The Glow seemed closer, but they weren't sure why. Nina just stared out over that great, raging sea and let the breeze glide across her face.

Before long the Watchers would arrive and that would be it. There were too many injured and the Watchers were too fierce. They would fight to the best of their ability, but it was going to be a massacre. There was a lot of crying and despair amongst the street-dwellers. But Nina noticed something else too.

She saw a young couple. They were a dirty, ragged pair of street dwellers with their knees in their chests and their heads resting on each other. There were tears in their eyes, but they were talking quietly in words she couldn't hear. They'd laugh for a moment and then wipe tears. She saw her kiss his bloodied and dirty face. The two just smiled and sat there with their eyes closed and their foreheads together.

Nina looked back at the Glow and felt some sense of thankfulness that if this was the end, that they would meet that end with full hearts. She was grateful for having tried even if it amounted to nothing.

It felt too soon when the Watchers started pouring out of the alleys and streets, closing in on the overlook. Many who weren't injured stood up to face them, ready to fight. Others stayed huddled with the groups of other street-dwellers they cared about. The Watchers kept getting closer. Fear was building, and there was more weeping and wailing. The Watchers had now formed a line and were about to charge. They made no call for surrender. No offers of mercy.

As Nina looked upon the hoard of Watchers, the wind started to pick up. It quickly went from a light breeze, to a heavy wind, to hurricane force gusts. Everyone including the Watchers had to huddle down. Nina looked behind her and saw two things she'd never imagined seeing. She could see almost the whole sea in front of her. The Glow was now almost to the shore of the dark city. She looked straight up and saw that the line between the darkness and the light was almost right above her head. She looked back at the sea and saw a bright white and majestic ship approaching.

The wind was intense. Before many could tell what was going on, the Glow met them with the fullness of its unbelievable force, followed immediately by perfect calm. All of the street dwellers were soon in the light. They were all looking around in awe. And though the wind was heavy, most of the street dwellers remained in place except for a few who tried to run. Those who tried to run away from the light were picked up by the wind and carried away. The majority of the Watchers tried to run from the light and were picked up and carried off though even some of them put down their weapons and stood firm.

The ship was nearly to the shore. Everyone was awestruck

by it. It towered above them, gleaming and glistening. No speck of rust. No dirt or wear. Simply perfect and beautiful in every way.

The overlook and ship came together as if always meant to meet. The crew of the ship extended the gangplank and started to offload, working feverishly, but not begrudgingly. None of them looked dirty. Their clothes weren't tattered. None of them looked angry or sad. They even waved and greeted the inhabitants of the dark city while they worked. The ship's crew was...friendly...and kind.... The words all started coming to them, but not like they were first learning them, but rather remembering them.

Finishing their work, the ship's crew lined up on either side of the end of the gangplank, saluting. The whole crowd began murmuring as someone started walking down it. He was dressed just like the ship's crew, except that he had a rather unassuming crown on his head. He didn't walk in any sort of pompous manner, nor pay much attention to the praise he was receiving from his crew. But he didn't stop to speak with the city's inhabitants just yet. He looked determined to get somewhere else first.

***

Dr. Ambrose calmly paced the aisles in his laboratory. He wanted as much Bright as possible, and he was unconcerned about the consequences, except one–that he be in control...of everything. And that goal would soon be achieved. Between the ramped up Bright production and the assault on the street-dwellers, he knew that he would not be deterred. The

Watchers were too well-trained, and the Bright was now too powerful and addicting. The street scum had no strength to repel even one, let alone both at the same time.

No one else in the room felt like he did though. Each of the Attendants were working feverishly, more so than before. They'd been working well past when they'd usually stop, and the lunch break was limited only to how long it took to scarf down a few bites. The beatings from the Watchers were harsher, more frequent, and for even the tiniest infraction. The looks of anxiety and deterioration were plainly evident on their faces. The work-product was beginning to suffer because of it, but it only made the beatings worse.

Dr. Ambrose took his leave and stepped onto the elevator to his penthouse. It crept up the floors with the same lack of enthusiasm it always possessed. It came again to a screeching halt, and the doors opened, but only slightly. The Attendant in the penthouse quickly came over and forced the doors open the rest of the way. Dr. Ambrose scowled at the Attendant as he stepped off of the elevator.

He stepped toward the record player, and placed the needle on the same old record. In his mind he truly wanted to enjoy it this time, but he still just hated it. He was frustrated with why that was so. After all, he was about to achieve all that he'd ever wanted to. There was no reason for him to continue disliking it, but he did. Dr. Ambrose left it on despite his continued disgust and walked toward the window to oversee the battle.

It was hard to tell what the tiny dots all over the city were doing, but he could tell just enough of what he needed to know by pacing back and forth along the window. That way he could see down different streets and alleys. Though he couldn't decipher all aspects of what was going on, he could tell that the Watchers were steadily advancing toward the shore. He could see the street trash retreating or dying.

He went and sat on his couch next to the record player and had no real success enjoying himself despite his victory. Never before had he tried so hard to tell himself that he was happy. Dr. Ambrose didn't stay seated for long before getting up and standing by the window.

"I have to squint," he thought with disgust. In denial that the Glow had now made it to shore, he refused to move.

What is this nonsense? Despite his indignance, and as much as he tried to resist it, the closer the Glow got, the more fearful he became. The building was shaking, and the windows started to crack. He took one step back and dropped his arms to his side. The light overcame the building. He fell to his knees as the glass shattered into thousands of tiny daggers.

***

As Blaise looked at the figure in the doorway, the rumble grew louder, and a heavy wind picked up. The Prince of the Deep Darkness dropped his sword and began letting out a piercing screech.

A booming voice then came from the figure in the door. It rang out loud, clear, and true.

"You who call yourself the Prince. Who darkens minds and casts hearts into shadow."

The figure stood stone still as the room rumbled again, and an explosion of light shot from behind him and pierced the room in every direction. The Prince and the Deep Ones had all fallen to their knees and were now gasping for air.

"For too long have you starved this city of all things right and pure."

Another rumble and explosion. The Prince and the Deep Ones were now fully collapsed.

"But today, your rulership ends. The veil will be lifted, for I have returned."

Blaise and Sally fell to the floor as a third rumble grew into a powerful earthquake. Blinding, continuous light now came from behind the man in the doorway. Blaise squinted trying to look toward him, and he could just barely see the same figure still standing unmoved in the doorway.

The screeching of the Prince and the Deep Ones was deafening. The Prince was now thrashing on the floor and appeared to be...crumbling. And he was. He was shattering into a million pieces before simply evaporating with all of the Deep Ones.

The earthquake stopped and the intensity of the light lessened. It was quiet, and the only three left were Blaise, Sally, and the man in the doorway. They looked around at where they were. It was beautiful and bright. The marble floors were glistening, the columns, the artwork, and the pews were all clean and dusted, and the place was filled with a light like they had never seen before.

The man in the doorway began walking down the aisle. Blaise let go of Sally's hand as they both turned toward him. He smiled at them, looked around the cathedral, and then breathed a cleansing breath.

"Morning is here."

Blaise didn't know what else to say. He paused for a moment trying to find any words he could. He felt a strange sense that no words he could say would be the right ones, though also that this man wouldn't pay any mind to indiscretions.

"Who...who are you?" Blaise finally stuttered.

"I am the King."

Blaise scratched his head in confusion. This man had obviously saved them from certain death and brought light with him, and for that he didn't want to seem ungrateful. Nor did he want to anger someone who no doubt held incomprehensible power. Yet still, something about the man gave Blaise confidence to ask a rather pointed question.

"If you're the King, where have you been?"

The King nodded in understanding at how Blaise felt before appearing to wipe tears from his eyes. Then he spoke.

"I have been across the sea in the capital of my kingdom."

His voice cracked in sadness. Before Blaise heard the crack in his voice, he had opened his mouth ready to go off in a frenzy, pelting this man with angry questions, but that stopped him. He went on.

"But, of course, you're not really asking out of curiosity, but because I stayed away, despite the achings in you that I would come near."

"But...but it was the Glow that I was after... not you. I've never met you," Blaise said.

"If you've sought the Glow, you've sought me, Blaise. I am its source. It is here. I am back."

"Back? You left?" said Blaise.

"Yes," the King said somberly.

Blaise still felt confused and a little angry and didn't know what to say. He just looked down at the shining marble floor glistening in the light.

"Why?" Sally said, finally getting up the nerve to say something.

"Because I didn't want to lose everyone when the city was swallowed in darkness," he responded. "If I had kept my light here, all would have been swept away."

Blaise looked back up at him, trying to understand.

"I wanted to have at all times been this city's ruler. But those here started to choose evil and darkness with their ways. I hated it, but allegiance demanded is not allegiance at all. I had two choices. I could have stayed and forced everyone to accept the light, but that itself would have been its own evil and darkness. It would have snuffed out all greater things...greater things like love. Love can only exist where there is the freedom not to love."

"What do you mean?" Sally said.

"Sally, you choose Blaise. Despite what difficulties come, you stand by his side, unwavering. If that wasn't your choice, if you'd been told by Blaise, or anyone else, that that is what you must do, it wouldn't be love. It would be slavery."

Sally nodded in understanding before the King continued.

"To stamp out love was inconceivable to me. It left me one other option: Leave the city in darkness. And though it saddened me to see the suffering and pain here, it was the greater option so that the light would not destroy them, but so they would have a chance to see the Glow. Though I didn't want the light to sweep any away, I knew that many would never turn back to it. So I waited. And here I am."

He had nothing else he could say to the King except

"Thank you." And though all that the King said was difficult to truly comprehend, he knew in his core that the King was indeed the King.

The King smiled. "Let us go back to the shore."

Blaise offered Sally his shoulder to act as her crutch despite his own aching leg, and to their amazement the King got on the other side of Sally to help.

"What kind of ruler is willing to do this?" they both thought. Blaise, Sally, and the King stepped out of the cathedral. It looked beautiful and bright now. He could see the ship well off in the distance docked at the overlook.

As they were heading back to the shore, joy filled Blaise and Sally with every passing step. They had been in a nightmare for so long, and now they were finally waking up. Their past existence felt more and more like a dream.

Sally's ankle began feeling strange, but slightly better. Confused but excited, she turned to the King.

"What's happening?"

The King then looked at Blaise with a joking smile before letting go of Sally. Blaise hardly had time to react to this, but somehow found that he trusted the King. Following his lead, Blaise let go of Sally too. Her eyes got wide and there was a look of betrayal in them. She anticipated the pain that would follow when her foot slammed to the ground. When it did, she grimaced and tightly closed her eyes, but the pain never came. She opened her eyes in confusion, looked at the King, and was elated.

"It's better!" She ran in circles around them. After a few laps, she stopped and looked at him again.

"It's not painful anymore, but why do I still feel a twinge like it's not quite right?"

"Do you see these buildings?" the King asked.

Blaise responded. "Yes. But...they're still rundown."

The King nodded in agreement.

"The city will still carry its scars, just like your souls, and just like Sally's ankle. The whole city and all of its inhabitants have gone through much, and it should not be forgotten. But I assure you that everything will recover and be made new."

A cool breeze passed by, and the King took in a deep breath and smiled.

They made it to the overlook in what felt like no time at all. Most of the city's inhabitants were now gathered there, celebrating, including a large number of Attendants. There was a buzz in the air—an excitement that had never entered into the minds of any. There were smiles on faces that had never worn them.

Blaise and Sally saw Nina, Bailey, and Carl. They all ran toward each other and hugged while the King went off in his own direction. Sally noticed that Nina's eyes were teary, but her smile was genuine. No words needed to be spoken. They all felt Parker's absence and the weight of it, but more than that they felt an indescribable peace.

Sally looked more beautiful than ever in the light. She was smiling and looking around at the crowd and the city. Blaise just gazed at her. And as he did, light filled his mind and he lifted his chin and straightened his back. Sally did the same thing at the same time. They turned toward each other and looked into each other's eyes. Big smiles came across both of their faces and at the same time they said the same thing. The thing they'd tried to say in the tunnel.

"I Love You!"

Though, in all fairness, Sally beat Blaise to it by a hair. Smiling was followed by laughing. Laughing was followed by crying. For a while crying and hugging accompanied each other. They looked at each other, wiped tears, and laughed some more. Blaise looked up and saw the King now standing on the bow of the ship, looking back at Blaise and Sally with a knowing smile.

Blaise noticed that a number of heads started to turn to see what was coming up the road. Nina was standing on her tiptoes trying to see, and the crowd started pointing and murmuring. Blaise turned and saw a large group of soot-faced and scraggly street-dwellers walking toward the overlook.

"The campfire men..." he whispered.

Nina heard him and turned.

"Who are the campfire men?"

"They wanted the light," he said, blankly staring in their direction

Unsatisfied with that answer, Nina decided to get a closer look. She started working her way through the crowd, shuffling sideways when needed and trying not to jostle anyone. She made it to the edge of the crowd and took in the peculiar sight. Ripped clothes, dirty faces, and long unkempt beards. But through those beards, they were smiling.

She smiled too before she noticed that one campfire man was carrying someone in his arms who didn't quite look like the rest of them. His head and arms were limp and his eyes were closed. Her heart started beating fast, and she felt like she was about to cry. She ran toward them as fast as she could. The campfire man put him down in front of her, bowed, and kept walking.

Kneeling down and holding his face, she tried to speak as softly as possible.

"Parker...Parker.... Please wake up."

She couldn't hold back tears.

"I'm right here. Talk to me. Say my name."

There was nothing. He was cold and motionless. She fell into his chest and cried harder than she ever had. As she did, she covered her eyes to block any light from coming in. And there she wept in darkness.

But as she did, she began to find it increasingly difficult to keep the light out. A few drops of light were creeping in between her fingers, and there was no way to stop it. It kept growing until she had no choice but to sit up and see what was going on.

Parker's body was now shining brightly. So brightly that she could hardly look. Light exploded from him, both knocking her back and cushioning her fall. The heat was intense but soothing, but both heat and light soon faded, and Nina watched as Parker inhaled and opened his eyes. Nina looked back at the King, standing on the bow. He was looking at her with the same smile that he had given Blaise and Sally.

Nina crawled back over to Parker as he continued to lay in the street. She took his face in her hands again but with happy tears.

"You...you gave your life for me."

Parker smiled.

"Because you're worth it."

A hush then came over the crowd and everyone turned toward the King. To Blaise, just the first four words he said were enough to breathe a life into him that he had never had.

The first word meant that he was not the sum of all his pain and mistakes. He was more than those things without deserving it. For the word was such that only the King could truly bestow it and to Blaise's astonishment the King did so freely, asking nothing in return.

The second word meant that he didn't merely exist. He was not just an empty accident doomed to breathe a few breaths and die. He was someone who possessed a value and dignity infinitely greater than what he or any other being besides the King could grant.

The third word meant that he belonged to something. He was no mere lonesome boy. Rather, he was a part, an important part, of something he now saw that he had yearned for since he first beheld the Glow, and which all who seek camaraderie, wonder, awe, and love long for: to be made whole by giving themselves to something greater.

And the fourth word was the name of that something: the city. But it was not a name that Blaise could fully wrap his mind around. Not in the old way when the meaning was hidden from him. Rather, now, the meaning was what resonated the loudest, though the name itself was infinitely beyond him.

"Good People of 'He uncovers the deeps out of darkness and brings Deep Darkness to Light'!..."

ABOUT THE AUTHOR

Ryan M. Jones lives in Richmond, Virginia with his wife, Shelby, and his three children. The Glow Across the Sea is his first novella. He also blogs, sharing other short stories and his thoughts on life and faith. He holds a Bachelor of Arts in Philosophy and Religion from Liberty University and a Juris Doctor from the Liberty University School of Law. In his free time he enjoys spending time with his family and playing the drums.

Printed in the USA
CPSIA information can be obtained
at www.ICGtesting.com
LVHW050230310723
753623LV00018B/1088

9 798218 222918